The Curse

Book One of the Nightshade Saga

By Brittany Burrus

Book 1 of 5

The Curse

Book One of the Nightshade Saga

Pronunciation Guide

Lilliana — pronounced LIL-ee-AH-nuh
Bellatrix — pronounced BELL-uh-tricks
Arachne — pronounced uh-RACK-nee
Ivy — pronounced EYE-vee
Zephyr — pronounced ZEH-fur
Lucas — pronounced LOO-kiss
Lennix — pronounced LEN-nicks
Sedrick — pronounced SAID-rick
Kelsea — pronounced KELL-see
Julian — pronounced JOO-lee-un
Amelia — pronounced uh-MEAL-ee-uh
Selene — pronounced suh-LEEN

Color and Symbol Index

⋈	TAN	Lilliana
⊘	GREEN	Ivy
⚶	RED	Bellatrix
◊	BLUE	Arachne

These are tools to use to make it more understanding. This book is purely fictional HOWEVER Dissociative Identity Disorder (Multiple Personality Disorder) is not a joke. I wrote this story as a better way to understand what some people experience; I drew inspiration from a close friend who prefers anonymity with their permission.

Author Playlist

One Day
Simple Plan

Ordinary
Alex Warren

Beg (On Your Knees)
Ash to Eden

Ruin My Life
Simple Plan feat. Deryck Whibley

Burn It Down
Linkin Park

Good Goodbye
Linkin Park feat. Pusha T & Stormzy

Our Forever
Spencer Crandall

I'm Your 911
Ruby Darkrose

Red Flags
Spencer Crandall

Chasing Shadows
Alex Warren

Trigger Warnings

Multiple Personality Disorder

Violence

Abuse (Verbal and Physical)

Possible Sexual Assault

Psychological Trauma

Mentions of Rape

Strong Language

Sexually Explicit

Possible Homicide

Kidnapping

Table of Contents

Prologue

Imagine a world of humans and magical creatures ranging from vampires, shifters, wizards, and witches. This is a story of Lilliana. A vampire princess that struggles with following her heart or doing her duty while juggling 3 additional people in her head.

Lilli really isn't sure who she can trust any more. Between doubting herself and the other souls she holds inside, who each want a different outcome. What is she supposed to do? Where is she supposed to go? Is she supposed to spend the rest of her immortal life wandering this bleak dark earth alone?

Chapter 1

Lilliana's POV

I'm wandering around the city of Seattle mindlessly. I don't have any place I'm trying to go, just trying to kill time and quiet the voices in my head. They are so damn loud I'm getting a migraine. It's the middle of August, you would think it would be scorching hot and sunny, but in all actuality, it's cloudy with a light drizzle of rain.

I prefer it this way, I absolutely love the smell of rain, plus the clouds help protect my skin from the sun. I'm a purebred vampire, sure I should just burst into flames and be scorched from any contact with the sun, but one of the perks of being born this way is I would have to be in the sun for a very long time. I also have a daily supplement that I take, courtesy of the magical community, which negates all effects from the sun for purebreds like me or even those that got turned.

I turn the corner and see a café that looks like it has few people in it. Good, I don't feel like dealing with other people today. I go in and wait in line to order a coffee before my phone buzzes. I look at it, I can't help but smile since one of my favorite people, Sedrick Moranth, sends me a message.

"Hey Lil, I was wondering if you want to do a double date with me and my girlfriend? I want you to meet her and see if she holds up to your liking. -SM"

I smile replying back, "Yeah! Of course I would love to meet your new girl. I'll ask Lennix if he wants to go. How about dinner tonight? We can go to Francesco's, we've always enjoyed eating there."

"It's a date doll, look forward to seeing you. -SM"

I finally get to the front of the line and look at the cashier. He is a little older than I figured he would be to work here. He looks me over, everyone does when it's the first time seeing me. I don't look like much. I'm not very tall, just below average at 5'4, with raven black hair and blood-red highlights mixed in, pale fair skin, and a slender frame with curves in the places that matter. I guess the only thing odd about my appearance would be my eyes.

I was born on a blood moon and was gifted with a rare occurrence of heterochromia. I've got one red eye, and one vibrant green eye. My mother says it's very rare to get red eyes when no parent has them. They said red is dark and twisted, an evil omen. My mother has blue-grey eyes, and my father has brown eyes, so getting the colors I've got shouldn't have been possible.

"What can I get you princess?" He asks, still checking me out. I shouldn't like the attention but the way his gaze sweeps over me makes me feel a warmth in my core. His voice is low but husky, he's got black hair and some silver mixed into it, he's relatively tall and well-built I can see his arm muscles through the tight shirt.

I smile, my fangs peeking out just a little, "I would like a coffee please, with a little bit of caramel cream." He tells me the price, as I go to hand him the money he grabs my hand gently. His hands are really warm, more than a human hand could be.

He looks into my eyes grinning, "So cold princess, are you sure coffee should be the thing to warm you up?" He takes the money with his other hand, rings it up handing me the receipt before turning my hand over and giving it a chaste kiss. "I look forward to seeing you again. Please, do come back."

I feel my cheeks heat, give him a quick thanks and go find a seat in the darkest corner. I reach into my backpack grabbing the book I'm reading, opening it to where my bookmark is, sit back, and read while waiting for my coffee. I barely get a page done when the cashier comes to sit down across from me putting my coffee down in front of me.

"What are you reading?" He asks, his low and husky voice making my core heat. I look up at him noticing his eyes are a shade of grey and sharp, waiting for a response.

I clear my throat to answer, "Just a fiction novel. It's called *Twisted* by Emily McIntire."

A voice in my head whispers, *you should not be talking to him. He isn't Lennix. We don't know him, you need to stop entertaining everyone you meet Lilliana.*

I shake my head a little but play it off like I'm cracking my neck, looking back at him with a smile. "I should get back to reading, thank you for bringing me my coffee and I hope you have a good day at work."

His eyes narrow as he looks at me before giving a curt nod, "Sure thing princess." He gets up and walks off, I watch for a moment wondering why his attitude changed before returning to my book.

I take a deep breath, finding myself unable to focus on the book. Retreating into my mind to visit the mindscape I created when I was younger. My physical body is fine for a little while since I move on autopilot while I'm inside.

Mindscape

It resembles an old wooden country cabin with 5 doors. The main door I enter through is in the front facing the main part of the cabin, a door to the west which has a grey-white wooden door, 2 to the south, one is oakwood, the other is bright cherry wood, and then there is the door to the east. This one looks like it's worn down, beaten, splintered in multiple places, and almost looks like it has been charred. I hear yelling coming from that room, going towards it. I get to the charred door opening it carefully; I duck in time to miss an object aimed at my face turning to look at who threw it. I let out a deep sigh, of course it had to be her. *"Bellatrix...what's got you so fired up now?"*

Her head whips into my direction, her eyes red and gold making it look like they have flames inside. *"You are too careless Lilliana! You should not be speaking to strangers all willy-nilly. You can get us all killed!"*

I look at the other 2 people in the room, they each mirror me except for the eyes. Arachne with her intelligent blue eyes, and Ivy with emerald-green eyes. They look like they are losing their patience, I need to diffuse the situation quickly. *"I'm sorry, I was only being friendly to the guy. Would it make you happier if I* relinquish control today and you go on a double date to see Sedrick?"

"*You would do that? For me...why?*" She looks at me, but I can see the rage in her eyes slowly starting to lose their intensity. It's working.

"*Because I don't need a migraine from hell when you rage out.*"

Ivy gets flustered and looks like she's frustrated about something, so I turn to her raising an eyebrow, silently asking her what's up. She grumbles before looking at the ceiling, "*I wanted to get out for a little while, I feel like I've been locked up, I've not been allowed out in ages, and it feels unfair.*"

"*Why?! You don't like to be out unless it's something for your gain! You go out of control, and I'm the one to suffer the consequences of it Ivy!*" I'm yelling, my body starts to tremble, I see Bellatrix starting to get fired up again. I take a couple slow deep breaths to try to calm my emotions. The others get triggered by different emotions I feel and sometimes forcefully take control. If I keep my cool, then maybe I can stay awake to see what happens when I'm not in charge.

"*Whatever Lil, you can go to hell and burn for all I care.*" She storms off and goes to her door that has the cherry-colored wood and slams it hard. A deafening click is heard which means she has sealed herself off for the time being.

I look back at Bellatrix stepping out of the door frame with an arm out letting her exit. *"Seat is all yours Trix. Please don't start any fires I'll have to put out."*

She heads to the singular door at the front and steps out without hesitation, I go to my grey door and step through, everything fades as I close myself off to rest.

Bellatrix's POV

Finally, it feels great to be in charge for once. I feel like I've been locked up for so long. I look at the coffee and drink it all in one go. It's not even hot anymore but it's not cold either. Looking around I see the cashier hard at work, I gather up my belongings, throw the empty cup in the trash, and head out.

I head home, going through our phone to see what I've missed out on. I see the message from Sedrick inviting us for dinner and smile, I send a message to our fiancé Lennix informing him about our dinner plans for a double date. "Hey, Sedrick invited us on a double date to meet his new girlfriend. It's tonight at Francescos. Would you like to join us? I miss you, love you."

I finally got home to a modest apartment complex. I live comfortably but not struggling, my fiancé stays over occasionally but he is an Alpha, so he mainly stays at his pack house. I don't want to live in the pack lands, too many werewolves on steroids. Been burned there before...I shudder as memories threaten to rise up, I give a slight growl, they skitter away.

I video call one of my best friends Lucas "Shadow" Bane, toss the phone onto the bed while waiting for him to pick up. He is currently traveling, trying to find a pack or clan that will take him in. He was born a werewolf, but when vampires attacked his pack when he was a child, he got turned before his first shift and became a hybrid. After a few rings he answers with a big goofy grin on his face, "Hey sweetheart! How are you doin?"

I laugh at his smile, it always warms a soul, regardless of how cold a person is. "It's going good big guy; I'm getting ready to take a shower and was checking in on my fluffy friend."

"A shower huh? Any chance I can get a show?" he wags his eyebrows seductively and I roll my eyes.

"No Shadow, you're not getting any shows. I'm in a relationship remember. I don't cheat on my partner."

He grumbles jokingly but shrugs, sitting under a tree leaning against it, "Can't blame a guy for trying. Especially knowing that fine body would be on display without an audience. I always hope you'll come to your senses and forgo societal acceptance."

I give out a laugh, rolling my eyes, "I was just calling to check in before I get in the shower. I have dinner with Lennix and Sedrick tonight with Sedrick's new girlfriend. How is your journey going?"

"It could be worse; I still haven't found the place I feel like I belong. One of these days though, no doubt about it. I miss you dearly, and all your bubbly sides. If you're calling me then I know exactly who it is," he winks before laughing, "I know you miss me too my beautiful Bella."

I grumble at the nickname; I hate it when anyone calls me Bella. I always go by Bellatrix or Trix, somehow Lucas is able to make me accept his nickname and I don't stop him from doing it. "Now I'm over it, bye Shadow." I flip him off and hang up laughing as he can't respond in time.

When I get off the phone Lennix finally responds back, "I'm sorry my dear, but no I won't be able to make it. There is an urgent matter I need to take care of in the pack. I'll see you tomorrow. -LW" I look at the message, my previously happy mood has now been dampened. I hate him skipping out on us again. It has been happening more and more often. Lilliana doesn't see it, but the rest of us do. I want to give him a fair chance, but he doesn't give us a lot of hope.

I hop into the shower, taking a quick one. When I get back out and check my phone, I see a message from Lucas that has the emoji of a middle finger multiple times. I laugh texting back with a red heart and go to Sedrick's messaging thread. "Hey, it will just be me tonight, Lennix has to take care of an emergency at the pack. I'll see you soon." I send it, getting dressed, I do minimalistic makeup with red eye liner and red lipstick, a red satin dress that shows my body frame off and clings snug but not too tight. Looking in the mirror, I hum in approval.

I walk to Francesco's a few blocks from the apartment. I get to the hostess desk, she leads me to a table, I order myself a glass of water while I wait for the others.

I hear a voice from behind while I'm looking towards the front door, turning to see the café cashier looking down at me. He's wearing a waiter's uniform and if I'm to be honest, he does fill it out nicely. I raise my eyebrow and look at him suspiciously, "Are you stalking me?"

He lets out a gruff sigh his eyes narrowed, "If anyone is stalking anyone, it's you. You've shown up to my place of work twice in one day, I don't know what bad karma I've got or if I pissed off a deity, but this isn't a pleasant coincidence in my eyes." He takes a deep breath and shakes off his grumpy look, putting on the fakest customer service smile ever. His eyes still look pissed, and I can't help but enjoy it. He gives me a look over, his eyes lingering on my cleavage. I don't try to cover but I do tap the table gently to get his attention. He clears his throat looking back into my eyes, "Hello, I'm Zephyr, I'll be your server this evening. What may I get for you today?"

Zephyr huh...I say the name a couple times in my head only to realize I quite like the sound of it. He pulls out a pen and his notepad ready to take my order. Checking the entrance then back at him I shake my head. "Nothing yet Zephyr, I'm waiting for 2 more people to show up for dinner. I'll just stick with water for the moment please."

He gives me a nod before he walks off; I watch him and tilt my head a little thinking what trouble he might cause. I feel something stir while I watch him making me feel unusual, so I quickly turn away and check my phone for messages. Seeing none I set my phone off to the side of the table.

Sedrick walks up to the table with his date. He has a smile on his face as he looks at me. I stand up to give him a hug. He is 6'11 with a stocky and well-built muscular body, shaggy hair and chocolate brown eyes. My hands can barely touch when I wrap my arms around his waist to give him a hug. He gives me a tight squeeze, kissing the top of my head before pushing me back a little to pull a girl to his side and introduces her. "Lilli, this is Kelsea, my girlfriend."

I smile, holding a hand out to her, she takes it gingerly and reluctantly like this was not something she wanted to do. "Nice to meet you Kelsea, I hope this oaf is taking care of you?"

She raises an eyebrow at me before shaking it off, giving me a smile so fake I'm surprised Sedrick didn't notice. "Nice to meet you to Lilliana. Sedrick has told me all about you. I couldn't wait to meet you." I hear a venomous tone in her voice and file that away for later. I'm not going to judge her until I get more information. I refuse to stand between Sedrick and his potential happiness. However, it doesn't negate the fact that I've got a very odd feeling about her.

We go through dinner making small talk, sharing stories about me and Sedrick from when we met and our adventures we've had after. I could swear I felt the table getting colder the more we talked about our history and could feel Kelsea wishing I was anywhere else. Zephyr does not linger at our table long during the meal, before Sedrick gets a chance, I grab the bill from Zephyr and pay for dinner smiling. The two of them leave and I get up after settling the bill. When I pick up the receipt I see a note on the bottom with a phone number saying 'Call me princess', rolling my eyes and stick it in my pocket heading home.

The walk home was a little chilly and dark. Night has fallen, taking a deep breath I relish in the brisk air. I'm almost home when I get the sensation of being watched. Stopping I look around, not seeing anyone on the sidewalks or street. I still feel that presence and it makes me uneasy. When I decide to continue walking, suddenly I feel my hair sticking up in the back of my neck warning me of danger. I hear a twang like a string has been snapped. I quickly drop to the floor, a wooden arrow embedded in the wall next to me. Looking up I notice a shadow of someone across the street on the rooftop holding a crossbow. They are staring at me with malice in their eyes.

I feel my blood boil, jumping to my feet running in a sprint, a perk of being a vampire is definitely having increased speed and agility. Jumping onto the rooftop, the figure tries to run away jumping between roofs, I chase them easily before suddenly I hear a deafening roar.

The sound is so loud I drop to my knees covering my ears tight, cursing my hearing for being so damn sensitive. My eyes squeezed shut from the pain until the roar dies out, I open my eyes to see a giant red dragon in front of me facing where the shooter went. I hear a pop as the figure disappears in a purple cloud magicking away.

Standing quickly, I end up regretting it as I get hit with vertigo causing my vision to blur. Trying to lower myself back down I end up toppling over, rolling down the roof as I begin to pass out. The last thing before falling is the dragon turning to look at me with silver dragon eyes and a snarl on its face.

Chapter 2

 *Bellatrix's POV*

I wake with a groan rubbing my head, safely laid onto the sidewalk I sit up slowly. Remembering what just happened, I look around frantically. *Where is the dragon?!* I see a shadow peering out from an alley behind my apartment. I jump to my feet and go after it, but by the time I reach it the shadow disappears and there's no scent to follow. I don't hear anything or anyone other than the city nightlife.

Hurrying into my apartment I lock my door. I rub my head, feeling drained, heading to my bedroom and get dressed for bed. I grab my phone sending Lennix a message before bed. "Hey, I just want you to know I got attacked on my way home from dinner tonight and passed out. I love you, heading to bed. Good night, Lenny."

I see 3 dots as he's typing his response, I wait for a few moments, and nothing gets sent. The dots go away, I take a deep breath plugging my phone in and going to bed.

Waking up I feel groggy, my head feels like it was kicked in, and the feeling of starvation is teetering close. Going into the kitchen I open the fridge, getting one of the blood packs, setting it in a pot of water warm up, putting it on a low heat.

Getting my supplement ready, I check my blood pack it feels perfect, I pour it in a glass and toss my supplement in my mouth before taking a drink of the blood. I shudder a little at the bitter taste, blood packs are sustainable, but it doesn't compare to feeding straight from the source. Taking my drink, I sit in my chair by the bay window, look out at the city. When I finish my drink, I put it in the sink, sitting back down in my chair retreating into our mindscape. *I need to talk to the others about what happened last night. They need to know about the dragon and the figure who shot at us.*

Mindscape

I walk through the front door, sitting on the charred wooden chair that matches my door. A round table sits in front of me, banging on the table loudly I yell out, *"Wake up ladies, we have a situation!"*

One by one each of them comes out of their rooms grumbling. Lilliana sees me sitting at the table and raises an eyebrow. *"What's wrong Trix?"* she asks as she takes a seat to my left.

Arachne takes her seat silently, arms crossed, ready to listen. Ivy takes the seat to my right. They all look at me curiously, I take a deep breath pinching bridge of my nose.

"I went to dinner with Sedrick and met his girlfriend. Her name is Kelsea, something does not feel right to me. I get a really bad vibe with her, and she seems to feel some sort of way about us." I start with the easy one.

Ivy is the first to speak which isn't shocking since Sedrick is the topic, ⌀ "Do you think she will try to keep him away? I won't allow another bitch to hurt him again!" She begins to rant before Lilliana bangs her hand on the table making it shake.

Ivy goes silent as Lilli speaks, ≈ "We all need to meet her individually to know if it's not just bias in regard to Sedrick."

I give a nod and take a deep breath, 🔥 "After dinner I got attacked, someone shot a wooden arrow from a crossbow, it barely missed because I was already on edge. I tried to chase them down, just when I was close to catching them, a red dragon interrupted me. He roared so loud it wreaked havoc on our ears, so I ended up fainting. When I came to, I was safely laid on the sidewalk, and the dragon was no-where to be found." Leaning back against the chair I rest my arms on the armrests.

Arachne straightens up leaning forward her hands holding each other with her fingers intertwined. 💧 "A dragon? Here in the city? They usually stay up in the mountains. I've not heard news of any of their kind coming out of hiding." She goes quiet, deep in thought.

Lilli scratches her head looking at the center of the table. ≈ "Did you catch the scent of the one who tried to hunt us?" Lilli looks at me hopefully since I've got the best intuition out of us.

I shake my head, sighing, 🔥 "they were masking it somehow, they definitely have to be a magic user. When the dragon got between us they vanished into a cloud of purple mist." One of our special talents is we can see peoples colors when they use magic, it's one of the quirks we received at birth.

🔥 "I don't feel like being out today, I feel weak and drained. One of you 3 need to take over. Keep a cautious eye." I get up from the table and go to my door shutting it.

Lilli looks at Arachne and Ivy before giving Arachne a pointed look. She gets up going to her room.

Arachne looks to Ivy, sighing, 💧 "You can take charge today, but please don't do something stupid. I can't keep shielding your transgressions." Without giving her a chance to respond Arachne goes to her room.

Ivy can be heard laughing as she runs to the front door going through it shutting it behind her completely.

🍃 *Ivy's POV*

Looking around I see we are just sitting in our pjs. I look out the window it's still morning, smiling I take a shower then get dressed. Decided on a green spaghetti strap tank-top, distressed black jeans, finding a black cardigan to go over it to cover from the chill wind. Slipping on a pair of black combat boots, grabbing my phone and backpack, before I head towards the café Lilliana went to yesterday.

It's busier than it was last night but seeming how it's still early in the day that's to be expected. I get to the counter seeing Zephyr.

He looks up at me, his demeanor changing. Before I got up there, he was friendly and nice to the other customers in the cafe. He took one look at me turning sour, "What can I get you today?" he asks in that husky grumpy tone.

I smile undeterred, "Hot chocolate please, with cinnamon syrup and whipped cream." He rings it up. I hand him the money, he gives me the receipt, I go back to the seat Lilli chose yesterday and sit there watching the busy café. I can't help but be drawn to watching Zephyr. Every now and then I catch his eyes finding mine. Winking at him I pull out the book in my bag, reading while I wait for my order. It didn't take very long before Zephyr brought my drink. He just sat it down, he was about to walk away when I reached out for his wrist.

His skin is warmer than most, I shudder involuntarily looking up at him. He stares at our hands, then locks eyes with me. I see anger as well as confusion. "Thank you for the drink. Care to join?"

He raises an eye brow, pulling his hand from mine, "2 things, 1 I'm at work, I'm busy, 2 I don't entertain games of hot and cold. So respectfully, I decline."

"I apologize, I like games, but I didn't mean to upset you. I would like to enjoy your company, plus you never know, I might surprise you. If you change your mind, I'll be here."

He blinks a couple times stunned, backs away going back to work. I catch him staring a couple more times while I'm reading. Hearing my phone go off I check it, seeing that it's Lennix responding to Trix's message from last night. "Good to hear you are safe, I'll see you later tonight. -LW" God I hate this guy, he is such a player and abuser. I ignore it, returning to my book.

I'm not sure how much time has passed before I get interrupted by Zephyr sitting next to me in a chair, reading over my shoulder. Looking at him from the corner of my eye, his eyes seem locked onto my book but for some reason I feel his stare. "Glad you can join me." I say, putting my bookmark in the book before putting it away in my backpack. He looks at me with those grey eyes shaking his head slightly to something.

He stands up offering a hand to help me up. I raise my eyebrow before taking it and he pulls me through the café out the back door towards a car. It wasn't anything fancy, just a '67 Cougar, with a black paint job and silver racing stripes. Looking over the car, I give a whistle of appreciation.

"I restored her myself, she's a beauty and very dependable." He opens the passenger side door, looking at me while leaning on the door testing me. "Come for a ride with me. I think we are due a conversation."

Giggling I grin, my fangs on full display, "Alright." I climb into the car tossing my backpack in the back seat buckling up. He shuts the door, gets in the driver's side, buckling, before pulling out of the parking lot. "So where are we going?" I ask while looking out of my window watching the city blur by.

"That's for me to know, and you to find out princess." He says smirking, his eyes on the road, left hand relaxing on the steering wheel, right hand on his shifter.

I look at him sideways checking him out fully. He is probably 6'7, slender muscular build, a clean cut short beard, his beard is more grey than black, which stands out in contrast to his hair which is mostly black with a little grey on the side. I notice that he has his right ear pierced with a blood red stone for the earring. His skin is definitely sun kissed, he looks like he could be a model...so why is he a cashier at a café and a waiter at night?

"Hmm." I see we're leaving the city, headed towards Mount Rainier. I don't say anything, but I'm on guard. I turn occasionally check to see what he could be doing. He still hasn't moved much except to shift gears when he needed to slow down or speed up.

After a while of driving, we pull up to a cabin close to the base of the mountain. Parking the car in front of the cabin he turns to look at me turning the car off. "We are here," he says holding the keys in his hand. "I hope you don't mind but I wanted this conversation to be private. There are a lot of prying eyes and unwelcome ears in the city. We're at my home. Care to join me for lunch? It would be appreciated." He watches me, checking to see if there's any fear from basically being whisked so far away from the city. Little does he know that I feel no fear, I don't fear him for I've met worse before.

Instead of answering I just get out of the car, heading to the front door without even waiting for him, I notice he has another car a few feet away, a 95 Jetta, solid black with dark tinted windows. I hear the car door shut behind me, he walks up when I reach the door. He unlocks it before stepping to the side. "After you," he says, stepping inside I look around. It's very minimalistic, with no décor, basic furnishings, and it's all dark and pristine. I see the entry to the kitchen, walking toward it, it's a very huge modern kitchen set up, Arachne would have a field day if she saw it. Taking a seat at the island on one of the bar stools I set my backpack down.

He's behind me the whole time, I could feel the heat radiating off him, being just close enough I can feel him but not so close that he's touching me. "What would the princess like to eat?" he asks while setting his apron on a hook, washing his hands.

"Why do you call me princess?" I look at him curiously. None of us have a princess-type persona, so I don't understand why he elicited that nickname for us.

He laughs turning to face me leaning back on the counter, both of his arms pressed against it. His previously tucked in work shirt now untucked. "I asked you what you want for food...and you choose to ask why I call you a princess. How curious." He smiles, I see humor in his eyes. "I call you princess because you have an aura of one, you carry yourself like royalty even though you may not look like one. You command the room without even trying, captivated my attention from just one look."

I look down and mumble to myself, *but that wasn't me...that was Lilli*, I say it low enough that he couldn't hear even if he was any kind of paranormal creature. "Surprise me. I'm not picky."

He tilts his head, like he's trying to get a read on me, "Alright, when we finish eating, I would like to ask some questions."

I watch him as he pushes himself off the counter, he moves around the kitchen with purpose. He starts cooking and I honestly have no clue what he could be making. After about 20 minutes he puts out two plates of chicken parmesan carrying them to the small dining table behind me. He sets them down, pulls out a chair looking at me. Walking over to him I sit in the chair as he pushes it in, then he sits to my left.

I look down at the plate of food, I won't lie, it looks delicious. I eat savoring each bite and was pleasantly surprised that the marinara sauce actually has a blood taste to it. "Is there blood in the sauce?" I ask him looking up for a moment.

He nods, finishing the food he has in his mouth before answering, "Yes indeed, I try to cater to other people's diets when it comes to cooking for more than myself. I hope it turned out ok for you?"

I eat some more while he's talking, nodding instead of answering back. When I finish my food, I notice he's already been done and has been watching me. Smiling I stand up, picking up our plates and taking them to the sink to wash them.

He slips up behind me, his hand brushing lightly against my back as he leans in, his lips close to my ear. "Princesses don't do the dishes." The words are soft, teasing, and before I can argue, he plucks the plates from my hands and sets them in the sink. His fingers curl gently around my arm, tugging me toward the living room. Dropping onto the loveseat, he crosses one ankle over his knee, his arm draped along the backrest with an easy grin, like he already expects I'll take the spot beside him.

I'm not one for close contact, it's too intimate, so I sit in the chair across from him. "So what questions are you wanting to ask?"

"First one is what is your name?" He's watching me intently.

Starting to say my name, I quickly correct myself, "I...I'm Lilliana. Lilliana Nightshade," I scold myself for almost sharing my name instead of our birth name.

"Try again. Please don't insult my intelligence by lying to me. I invited you to my home to be free of ears for both my comfort and your own." He says sitting straighter with both feet now on the ground with his arms crossed to his chest.

"It's the truth. That's the name I was given when I was born." I can feel my chest getting tight, worried I fucked up by stumbling on my name.

"That's the name the body was given, but not the person I'm speaking to. So, I ask again, what is YOUR name?" He's even more rigid than before, I'm strangely compelled to answer him. *I don't feel like he would harm me in any way, but should I trust my intuition and tell him? Or should I tuck tail and run back to the city like any other sane person would?*

"Ivy," I finally answer not making eye contact, looking out the window. It is raining, it looks like it's coming down pretty hard. *Trying to escape could prove challenging.*

"Ivy.... Well, that's a name fitting for a princess for sure. Tell me Ivy, are there other people that possess your mind?" Leaning back to his relaxed state, watching me, his stare is intense and heated. I'm sure if I was human I would combust under pressure.

I shrug, *no point in lying*, "yes, 3 others. 4 in total." I turn looking into his eyes, but I don't see rejection or disgust, I see awe and curiosity.

"That makes sense, given what's happened the last 24 hours then. I assume I've met 2 others then you?" I nod, "hmm interesting, tell me princess. Why did you come with me? It could be dangerous, I could be a serial killer leading you to your doom. Out here in the mountains no one can hear you scream, not capable of out running me."

Laughing internally, I respond, "You shouldn't underestimate me Zephyr," standing up I cross my arms, my eyes narrow. *He thinks I'm weak*, that gets my blood boiling. "I can handle myself just fine, I don't feel like I'm in danger here. If you're going to be a dick, then I'm just going to show myself out and walk back to the city." Grabbing my backpack I head towards the door.

As my hand reaches the handle, a small smack is heard as he slams a hand on the door stopping me from being able to open it. Standing behind me, his breath can be felt on my head. Leaning down to my shoulder, his breath on my neck he softly whispers, "Don't leave. I know you can handle yourself, I've seen it. I'm just trying to gauge your survival instincts. I don't like carelessness."

As he finishes talking, I grin knowing he is exactly where I want him. Turning around slowly my face is inches from his. I stare into his grey eyes. He puts his other hand on the other side of my head caging me against the door, not physically touching me.

Chapter 3

Leaning against the door watching him, I see him wondering how I'm going to react to potentially being caged. *I'll let him make the first move. I want to see how far he plans to go.*

He takes the opportunity to look down at my cleavage, he's got the perfect view, his body tenses up. *Alrightie, it looks like he likes what he sees, so let's see what he's got.*

"I'm not scared of you Zephyr, if I wanted to leave, I can. You couldn't stop me if you tried." I lunge at his neck, my fangs ready to pierce, he moves backwards shock on his face. Taking the opportunity, I run around him, back towards the kitchen. I can hear him taking off after me, running through the house looking around quickly. Finding the bedroom with a door to the back of the house that leads to the forest lining the bottom of the mountain.

Stopping to enjoy the view, I didn't even hear him before he pushes me face first into the glass door pinning me there.

Letting out a grunt I push against him hard, he stumbles a little before recovering, grabbing my waist and pins me back against the glass with his body pressed against me. I'm breathing slowly and deep, frustrated at myself for getting distracted easily.

He leans down, his mouth close to my ear, "I won this little race you chose to have. What prize should I receive?"

"No bet was placed, Plus I don't know what kind of prize you want. So, if you really wish to have a prize, you will have to claim it."

Moving my hair out of his way, he inhales my scent letting out a frustrated groan. "The prize should be you, I want to devourer you, make you come so many times that your body shakes every time I touch you." He presses a kiss to my neck, his hands still holding me firmly to the glass.

As he kisses my neck my body stiffens. I whisper in a heavy breath, "then do it, what's stopping you?" I challenge him.

I can feel his control snap, he quickly spins me around, grabbing my hands holding them above my head pinning them there. As he stares into my eyes, his look darker and hungrier. Arching my body towards him urging him to touch me. My eyes wander to his lips, wondering when I'll feel them on mine.

"Once I start, I won't stop." He tightens his hold on my wrists, making it so he can keep them pinned with one hand, his free hand trails down my arm slowly, gently puts his hand on my neck using his thumb to lift my chin up.

"Who said I wanted you to stop Zephyr?" Pushing against his hold, I arch into him, desperate for more of his touch.

The last bit of self-control has disappeared, he slams his mouth to mine kissing me, his tongue pokes at my bottom lip demanding entrance. I open my mouth inviting him in kissing him back. His hand that was on my throat trails down to my tank top pulling it up, cupping my breast, kneading my breast and twisting my nipple.

Letting out a soft moan into his mouth, I squeeze my legs shut as my core starts to throb. He trails kisses down to my neck biting without breaking the skin. He releases my hands above my head to pull my cardigan off tossing it to the floor. He looks at me, "Last chance to back out princess."

I'm breathing hard, staring at him. Instead of answering I grab his shirt, yanking it off his head tossing it with my sweater. He presses me against the glass pulling my bra and tank-top off giving him full access to my breasts which are perky, firm, and a manageable size.

Leaning down he bites the top of one breast, kneading the other roughly, licking my nipple pinching it with his fingers. His other hand trails down my body to my pants, with one fluid movement he has them unbuttoned and unzipped. He pushes his hand in them and feels how wet I am.

He groans in appreciation while continuing to assault both of my breasts with kisses, licks, and bites. He slides his middle finger in between my folds finding my clit. My eyes close, biting my lip as I lay my head back against the glass. He starts to move his finger in slow circles, causing a moan to escape. He pushes my pants down with his free hand, still stimulating my clit teasingly. The pressure builds as my orgasm nears.

Before I have a chance to react he reaches under both of my thighs with his arms, lifts me up my legs now resting on his shoulders, my pussy in his face, it's wet and inviting. Looking up at me, he grins, "Oh, this is going to be delicious. So wet and juicy, I sure hope you're ready for this."

He dives his head between my legs, his tongue swirls circles on my clit, he has one hand spreading my folds for entrance. He slides a finger in slowly, feeling how tight it is, he gives an amused laugh while continuing his assault on my sensitive bud pumping his finger in and out. Arching my back, I moan louder, my hands in his hair gripping tight.

My orgasm builds as he darts his tongue in me, swirling it around, he adds another finger pumping them in and out as his tongue goes back to my clit. My body shakes as I get close to my orgasm. I grip his hair tighter moaning louder. He bites my inner thigh while still fingering me deep and fast.

The bite is all it took for my orgasm to rip through me, causing me to moan loudly. When the high of my orgasm starts to disappear, I pull his hair roughly lifting his head, "your turn."

He looks up at me grinning, "That's not how this works princess. Besides you're not in any position to make any demands."

Giving him my best pouty face I let out a small whine, "I want to taste you, shouldn't a princess get what she wants?"

"Some princess's do but I'm not done by any means," he pulls his arms from under my thighs lowering me back down and kisses me hungrily. Tasting myself on his tongue I groan kissing him back with just as much intensity.

He has a nicely toned body. I run my fingers over his chest feeling faint scars over them trailing my hands to his waistband, unzipping his pants. "I can go for a while Zephyr, please indulge my cravings." I slip my hand into his pants and boxers, I feel his erection straining to be free. Keeping eye contact with him giving a small squeeze to his dick with a grin when he grunts.

"By all means, show me what you got princess," he stares at me with heat in his eyes, grabbing a fist full of my hair encouraging me to drop to my knees.

I slowly go to my knees pulling his pants and boxers with me, his erection springs free. He isn't big by any means, but what he lacks in girth, he more than makes up for in length... *can he even fit in me completely without ripping through my cervix?!*

I give a teasing lick to the tip running my tongue up and down the length of him. I cut my eyes up to look at him, he is watching me intensely. I take him in my mouth slowly bobbing my head back and forth, taking more of him in each time till he reaches the back of my throat realizing I haven't even reached his base yet. Bobbing my head faster, one of my hands cups his balls massaging them.

His breathing picks up, I prepare myself to open my throat, forcing his cock in more till my lips reach his base. Tears tickle the corners of my eyes as I start to choke, but I don't stop...I continue moving. I don't want to stop, I crave him losing control. His hands tighten in my hair as his head rolls back, he groans moving my head taking control, shoving himself deeper into my throat. Tears run down my face as I choke, I can feel his dick twitching as he gets close. He continues the assault on my throat, groaning as his body shakes. He bursts in the back of my throat.

I swallow every drop, licking him clean. Pulling back with a pop I look up at his satisfied face. His dick softens, but when he looks at my eager face he starts to harden again. He pulls me up roughly by the hair. "That was fucking amazing Ivy. I need more of you." He kisses me hard like he's trying to devour me, picks me up by my ass slamming my back against the glass. He moves his mouth to my neck, gives me a rough bite, spreading my legs to position himself at my entrance.

I wrap my arms around his neck, gripping his hair as he kisses and bites on my neck. "Take me," I whisper out, that was all he needed to slam himself deep inside me. I moan out in pain and pleasure at the rough entrance. Laying my head back against the glass as he pounds in and out of me with no mercy, at a pace I would think rabbits would be jealous of. I'm moaning loudly due to the continuous pounding, our skins slapping against each other. My orgasm builds and my breathing picks up.

He releases one hand off my ass using it to grab my throat, pulling my face to his while squeezing just enough to hurt but not enough to cut off air. He kisses me deeply, continuing his assault on my pussy. Moaning into his mouth as my orgasm rips through me, my walls clamping down on his dick. He moans into my mouth thrusting himself a couple more times before slamming as deep as he can go, letting go of his own orgasm.

My breath is heavy and fast, he holds me in place breathing heavy as well. He releases my neck, moving his hand back to my ass carrying me to the bathroom attached to the bedroom. He carries me into the shower and gingerly sets me on my feet turning the shower on.

The water is warm, feels great spraying on my skin. He turns me so my back is against his chest, he wets my hair, washing it for me. I'm unsure what to think as he just fucked my brains out and now is pampering me to clean me up. I'm not used to this so I close my eyes, letting him wash my hair, rinsing it out. He gets a washcloth with some bodywash, washes my body, being gentle cleaning every inch of my body. He puts me under the water to rinse off, I hear him moving, turning to look at him after I finish rinsing off, I see he's washing his own body.

When we are done, we dry off and get dressed. I put my clothes back on as he changes into dark jeans and a loose-fitting tank top. He watches me the whole time I get dressed. Clearing my throat, I go back to the living room, sitting on the chair I chose earlier. He's not far behind me, sitting back on the loveseat with his arm resting against it.

The silence between us drags as we look at each other. I feel satiated, the look on his face tells me he feels the same.

"Well, that was an interesting turn of events. When I brought you here, I was not expecting anything like this to happen. In fact, I wanted to learn more about you and the other souls that live within you." He says smiling as he looks at me, I can see there's more to it, but I'm not going to push yet.

"Ask your questions, no lies this time." I cross my legs, putting my hands in my lap watching him.

He taps the back of the couch contemplating, then holds his hand out, motioning for me to come sit next to him. "First thing first, sit with me. I would like you close."

I debate for a bit before getting up, I sit next to him, my back to the arm of the couch laying my legs across his lap facing him, my arms crossed on my chest. He puts his arm across my legs gently rubbing them up and down. "My first question would be why did the others reject my company?"

"Because we are engaged to someone, and they don't cheat on our partner. They have a different moral compass in that regard." I watch his hands because I don't want to look in his eyes and see judgement for what we just did or learning I cheated on our partner. "Lilliana, the one you met at the café, she is our 'birth' soul, she came with the body when she was born. She's a kind and loyal person, will befriend anyone. Bellatrix, the one you met at the restaurant, is our protector. She has a mean streak and can come off as very rude. She won't step out on our partner unless she no longer feels loyalty to them."

As he is listening to me talk, he watches carefully, I still avoid eye contact. "Why do you act differently?"

Taking a deep breath, I rub my arms, tugging them closer. "I don't believe in relationships. I believe in living life to the fullest, doing what feels good and right.

Despite what society says is acceptable. I am reminded often that I lack a moral compass, and the ability to care much about other people's feelings." I finally look at him after admitting the truth, surprised he's not looking at me differently. If anything, he seems almost amused.

Grinning still rubbing my leg, "So you don't care about others, yet you wanted to reciprocate when I ate your pretty little pussy out. How does that make sense princess?"

Letting out a dry laugh, "I'm a very sexual person. I don't consider people's feelings, but I love watching those I have sex with lose control, lost in the same pleasure I feel. It's purely a selfish reason for me to reciprocate. I only care about certain people's feelings after I developed a certain connection with them."

He's watching me silently thinking about what I said, "Well, you won't hear me complain about it, in fact I would love to do this again sometime." As he continues rubs my legs he looks at the clock behind me on the wall, "I guess I should get you back to the city. I gave Bellatrix my phone number yesterday. Any time you want to have fun, don't hesitate to reach out and shatter my self-control. Maybe put in a good word so I can have fun with the others," he says with a wink.

"Don't count on it. As long as the others are committed to Lennix, they won't even look at anyone else." I consider my words after I say them, "Well except maybe Arachne, she doesn't like Lennix, never has. But she will consider the outcomes of everything before giving into her whims."

Moving my legs off him, he stands up, offering me a hand. We head back to the car and start the drive back to the city. He doesn't ask for directions, so I assume he is taking me back to the café. After about an hour's drive, he pulls up in front of my apartment, making me look at him warily, "How do you know where we live?"

Clearing his throat, he gets out of the car walking to my door, opening it for me offering me his hand. Refusing his help I get out, putting distance between us, still waiting for an answer. "It's not what you think Ivy..." without letting him finish I turn my back, going inside quickly locking the door.

Putting my bag away, I check my phone, no messages. heading to the chair by the window, A knock is heard before I sit, opening the door I see Zephyr standing there with a frown.

"Please let me explain before you slam the door in my face. I swear I'm not going to harm you in any way," he pleads, holding his hands up in surrender.

Glaring at him I turn walking away, leaving the door open. I sit in my chair my arms crossed on my chest. He enters the apartment, shutting the door behind him. Sitting in the chair across from me, he looks around at the apartment. It's got the two high back chairs which we are sitting in, a small couch, wooden coffee table with mail scattered over it, a standard kitchen, and no tv.

"I'll give you five minutes to explain before I throw you out ending this game you are playing."

He gives a nervous smile, nodding, "After Bellatrix left my shift was over, I was headed back to the café when I saw her walking about 40 feet ahead of me before she dropped to the floor. She jumped up quickly, taking off to chase the figure that shot her. I didn't think...instinct took over I knew I had to act so I shifted and tried to help. She saw me in my dragon form but fainted after the figure disappeared." Taking a deep breath, he rubs his hands together nervously. "She started to roll off the roof, I managed to shift, catch her, and laid her on the sidewalk. When she started to wake I hid in the nearest alley, to avoid confrontation. Don't get me wrong, I feel guilty for disappearing, but I made sure she was safely inside and turned the lights off before I left.

My jaw drops, staring at him in awe, "You are the dragon that Trix told us about?" Closing my eyes I access her memory events, seeing the dragons silvery eyes. Opening my eyes I look at Zephyr with his grey eyes. "That's not possible...dragons aren't supposed to be here. They are private creatures."

Giving a heavy sigh rubbing his forehead he nods, "We usually are, but I crave connection, whether it's physical or emotional. I've been alone for a very long time," he pauses looking at me knowingly, "isolation isn't all it's cracked up to be."

He puts his hands back in his lap rubbing them, "I enjoy working some sort of customer service, I like seeing people smile at the fact someone is trying to cheer them up every day." Smiling he looks me over, "It was all going smoothly, until a certain pale faced vampire walks into my café with the most captivating eyes I've ever seen. Secrets loomed under the surface of her eyes; I craved the challenge to uncover them. I admit my ego did not like being rejected but now understand why. I'm sorry I didn't tell you the truth, I deal with a lot of judgement for being a dragon... it causes disfunction."

Laughing I uncross my legs watching as his eyes drop to them. "I understand not wanting to open up. We are the same. I appreciate you telling the truth. Not trying to be rude, but you need to leave so I can talk to the others. It's a lot to handle. Please give them time."

He nods as he stands, walking to me. He presses a kiss to my forehead, "Till next time princess."

After he leaves I lock the door, going to the bedroom laying down, checking my phone. I notice Lennix, Sedrick, and Lucas sent a message. Ignoring them I close my eyes going into the mindscape while our body rests.

Chapter 4

✿ Mindscape

Taking my seat at the table, I see Arachne pacing in the room. ✿ "What's wrong Ara?"

When she sees me, she relaxes. Sitting in her chair, she folds her arms like normal, ◊ "I was getting worried because you blocked us. Not knowing what you were doing has Lilli freaking out. So, what have you been up to?"

Suppressing a laugh I smile, ✿ "Nothing much, went to the café and ran into Zephyr. He could tell something was different about me when I was in charge and felt like Trix and Lilli were giving him whiplash all day yesterday. So, we talked, learned each other better. Turns out he also is the dragon Trix told us about."

Ara narrows her eyes, looking at me with a glare, ◊ "What does he know Ivy?"

✿ "Everything, I told him cuz it was pointless to lie, he could see through me. He isn't dangerous, in fact he's actually very nice and understanding to us." Looking away I decide to keep the activities we had a secret, *it's my personal memory and the others don't need to know.*

She shakes her head, yelling for the others to join us. They come out of their rooms, joining us at the table. Ara speaks first, ◊ "Zephyr, the guy from the café and restaurant, is the dragon Trix saw last night. He also is privy to our truth, he knows about ALL of us."

Lilliana blanches looking like she's going to throw up, "what the fuck are you talking about? Why...how the fuck does he know?!" she looks at me but I just shrug.

"I'll take over for the rest of the day," she says heading towards the door before Ara smacks the table hard enough it sounds like a gavel.

Ara follows her, grabs Lilli's arm stopping her from touching the door. "You need to calm down and cool off. You are in no shape to handle things rationally. I'll handle things today, you need to stop trying to control everything all the time, trust in us to handle things. Stay in your room while I get to the bottom of this."

Lilli glares at me, her gaze would scare others, but I'm not fazed. She yanks her arm away, storming off to her room slamming the door shut causing the rest of us to cringe. Ara turns to me sighing, "What's the status with Lennix?"

Looking at her, I shake my head, "He messaged this morning responding to the message Trix sent but he didn't show any worry about the attack. He said he would see us tonight. Why do we continue to deal with him? He's abusive, controlling, and he's been neglecting us for years. He works too much, never has time for us. I think it's bullshit."

Ara nods, heading to the door, "Privacy." She says before shutting it completely making everything dark as Trix and I get thrown into our rooms with the doors slammed shut.

◊ *Arachne's POV*

Slowly opening my eyes, I sit up rubbing my head. I head to the kitchen, grabbing a blood pack from the fridge and dropping it into a pot of water on the stove while checking my phone. Grumbling to myself seeing the unread messages, ◊ *damn it Ivy, why the fuck would you leave all this for us to deal with?* I open Lennix's first.

"Hey, I'll see you tonight at the café shop down the street from your place. I need coffee, you can read while I do my paperwork. See you at 7. -LW"

I type up a quick reply, "Alright babe, sounds like a date. See you soon, I love you." Opening the message from Lucas, it was a picture of him standing on the edge of a cliff looking down at the ocean, wearing nothing but board shorts. Laughing I send him a blue heart emoji with a kissy face, before opening up Sedrick's.

"Hey doll, I think dinner went well. What did you think of Kels? She said she thinks you are alright and likes you." I laugh, he's blind as a bat which is shocking since he's a fucking were-bear.

Considering my reply, I respond back, "I think it went well too. She seems nice, look forward to doing it again bud. I'm going on a date with Len so I've got to go for now. Talk to you later." I check the time it's 6pm, my blood is warm, I've got enough time to drink it and change. ◊ *Maybe I can get there early and test the atmosphere.* Pouring the blood into a glass, drinking carefully as I walk to the bedroom, pilfering through the closet. I find a navy-blue dress that makes my pale skin look paler. I finish my drink, setting it down on the dresser before slipping the clothes Ivy wore off. I put the dress on, loose and wavy, just how I like it. I brush my hair, put a little bit of black eyeliner on. Grabbing a black blazer as I head to the door, grabbing my backpack and phone. When I open it, a man is there looking like he was about to knock.

Based on what the others have said this must be Zephyr. Smiling sheepishly, he looks at me, "hey, sorry I was about to knock. I wanted to see you before I went to work, they called for some help."

My arms fold across my chest, drawing his attention to my breasts. I clear my throat which makes him look back in my eyes, "I'm headed out. I have a date with my fiancé."

"Ahh, sorry I don't mean to interrupt. By all means, lead the way princess." He gives a bow holding his arm out, rolling my eyes I shut and lock the door.

While walking down the street I notice he stays next to me, close enough I can smell him but not so we are touching. "So, who do I have the pleasure of speaking to now?" He asks, "I can tell you're not Ivy."

Freezing in place, I give him a fierce glare, "No, I'm not. YOU may call me Arachne in private. But when we are out in public, we are all Lilliana. She should not have told you about us." Continuing walking, I grumble to myself. He opens the door for me.

He jumps right into work as I get in line. I keep my eyes on him, curious why Ivy was suddenly private when discussing him. Reaching the counter he smiles at me amused, "Hello, welcome to Caffé Vita, what may I get started for you today?"

Putting on a fake smile I place my order, "May I please get a hot chai tea?" Telling me the total, I pay, and he winks as he hands me the receipt. Going to our table in the back, sitting down as I pull out my phone checking the time. ⬦ *It's only 6:30, Lennix should be here soon.* Someone drops off my tea, sipping it I scroll on my phone waiting for Lennix.

After a few minutes I hear Lennix's voice cut through the crowd, Zephyr is smiling, being his good customer service self. Lennix seems to be acting like a difficult customer, but Zephyr handles it well, he pays for his stuff, waits for his coffee at the counter then joins me at my table, sitting across from me. He gives me a fake smile kissing my cheek quickly before he pulls out paperwork.

We sit in silence, he works while I drink my tea. After about 20 minutes I've had enough of the silence. "What's wrong Len, why are you pretending I don't exist? Did I do something to upset you?"

He grumbles before setting his stuff down looking at me, "Stop overreacting Lilliana, you're reading into things, I'm just busy. Your acting very insecure."

"Insecure...overreacting...hmm," Finishing my tea I stand grabbing my bag. "Go to hell and rot Lennix Wolfe." I leave, managing to make it outside before my wrist is grabbed in a death grip by Lennix. When I try to pull away he growls squeezing tighter.

Glaring with fury in his eyes, "don't walk away from me again Lilliana. I won't tolerate disrespect." He pulls me forcibly down the sidewalk, we reach his Charger, he yanks open the door pushing me towards it, "Get in."

Knowing it's easier to list I get in quickly without arguing, he slams the door hard shaking the car. When looking out the window, I see Zephyr is out front looking around. He starts walking towards the car seeing Lennix's rage. I avoid looking at him as Lennix gets in the driver's side, ripping away from the curb. He zips through traffic, grumbling I can feel fury radiating off him making me nervous.

◊ *This isn't going to be a good day.* We pull up to an isolated cliff, he turns the car off after putting it in park. He pushes his seat back, unbuckling himself, grabbing my hair roughly. "What makes you think you can walk away like that Lilliana? You know better." He holds my hair firm, there's anger in his eyes but I notice the bulge in his pants.

I put on the fakest smile I can muster knowing what to say to calm him down. "I'm sorry Lenny I shouldn't have walked away or been disrespectful, please forgive me?" his fingers loosen in my hair, I lean forward kissing him softly.

He pushes me away and gets out of the car, walking to my door and opens it holding his hand out. "Get out."

Clearing my throat, I take his hand and stand, he turns me around and presses my head down pushing my head back into the car over my seat. "I forgive you, but you still need punished. Be a good girl and stay still." He says as he slides my underwear down my dress.

I close my eyes hoping it's just his spankings he likes to dole out and not anything else. I grip the seat tight ready for whatever's to come. I can hear him undo the zipper of his pants and my eyes snap open. *I won't allow him to keep treating us like this. I allowed it for too long.* When I feel him get closer I look at my backpack and grab the strap tightly. He rubs my ass cheek lightly before smacking it so hard I jolt forward into the car, my knees hitting the bottom of the door frame. I try to straighten myself up but my feet slip on the gravel causing me to drop hard to my knees.

Lennix grips my arm and pulls me up hard, I take the opportunity to shove him hard away from me causing him to get thrown a couple feet away into the road skidding into a tree. I quickly pull up my underwear and grab my back pack walking down the road back to the city.

He's cursing, yelling for me to come back, as I walk down the road. He chases after me tackling me into the street causing my dress to rip in in a couple places. Gravel gets stuck into my cheek as he yells, "Get the fuck back here bitch! YOU'RE MINE. Where the fuck do you think you're going?!"

Headbutting him as hard as I can to knock him back, he falls backwards. I stand facing him ready to fight.

"I don't belong to anyone Lennix Wolfe. You don't own me. I've allowed your behavior to go on for so long, but I'm done. We are over. Come after me or touch me again...and I won't think twice about killing you."

He jumps to his feet fuming, his nose bleeding from when I smashed my head into his. His hands turn into fists, his wolf just under the surface threatening to take over. "You fucking bitch, you're stuck with me. Your parents pushed us together, they won't stand for this. I will not allow you to fuck everything up!"

Sighing heavily, picking up my backpack dusting off the loose gravel I look at him, "Looks like you will have to figure it the fuck out yourself. I'm done letting you treat me like a punching bag. I'm a person, not a thing you can toss around."

Walking down the road, my back to him, I hear a loud growl, bones snapping. He's shifting hoping to scare me in submission, unbeknownst to him I'm not scared of him, he uses it to scare Lilli. Paws are hitting the concrete, getting closer, I choose to sidestep at the right moment when he lunges past me. Looking at Lennix's wolf, I stare into its eyes, he's huge, his fur is pitch black and his eyes are just as dark.

A car is heard getting close, his head whips to the sound. He sprints to his car, shifting back, he glares at me with hatred. "This isn't over Lilliana!" Climbing into his car he pulls out of the parking spot quickly, tries to run me over as he speeds down the middle of the road, but I jump over the car easily. He barely misses the car coming around the bend.

The approaching car pulls up next to me skidding to a stop. Looking I see it's Zephyr. He slams the car in park, rushing to me checking me over. Other than a scrape on my hands and knees that is in the process of healing there's no damage. "Arachne are you alright baby?" he cups my cheek after brushing gravel off my face.

◊ *Baby...did he just call me baby?* "I'm fine," Dusting off my ripped dress I look up at him, "Can you give me a ride back to my place please?" Going to the passenger side door of his car, I was about to open it when he reaches in front of me opening it. Getting in I put my hands in my lap watching them heal. He gets in the driver's seat, we sit in silence for a few minutes, he starts to drive but I'm not paying attention to where we are going.

Taking advantage of the silence, I reach into our mindscape opening the door just enough so that the others can communicate with me now. ◊ *We have a problem, Lennix attacked me. I am fed up, I broke up with him, and we need to prepare for our parents to be upset.* Looking out the window, I notice we are leaving the city.

Trix perks up first, 🔥 *are we finally done taking bullshit from him?*

I let out a small hum as an answer. Lilliana starts her inevitable rant, *Wait what?! Why did he attack you? Why would you break up with him for it? What do you mean abuse Trix...he loves us it's not abuse if we deserved the punishments we got.* I can feel her presence getting agitated and nervous.

◊ *He attacked us because I had enough with his bullshit treatment. I got into his car fully intending on waiting for him to cool off when he pulled up to a cliff and tried rape me. I shoved him and walked away instead, so he tackled me, said a whole bunch of shit after I busted his nose. When I walked off I said we are finished then he shifted. His own wolf tried to attack me and force me into submission. When he heard another car coming he drove off trying to run me over in the process. Zephyr picked me up, we are driving to his place now. Just opened up to let you know what is going on. Leave me alone.* Pulling the door closed again I close my eyes enjoying the drive.

Before long we pull up to his place, he gets out jumping over the hood to open my door before I can. He holds a hand out to help me up, I hand him my bag instead. Getting out of the car, walking to the door I wait for him. After he opens the door I look around deciding to head to the doors leading out back. Opening the door, sitting on the bench that sits to the side of the deck with a table and 2 chairs against the house. Zephyr follows, he tosses my backpack on the couch as we pass it, joining me on the bench.

"Why did you bring me here?" I ask, looking at the small river that flows nearby.

"Because I needed to make sure you were ok. You took off in a hurry, the big guy looked pissed, then you got into the car I had a bad feeling. So I grabbed my car, tried to catch up." He gently takes my hand, pulling it closer to turn over, checking my now healed palm. "May I ask what happened princess?"

Watching our hands together I shake my head. "Not anything for you to worry about. I can take care of myself. But thank you for asking." He folds his fingers into mine sighing. Letting go of his hand I grab his chin, leaning forward kissing him letting go of restraint.

He closes his eyes kissing back, one of his hands cupping my jawline. Using his free hand, he pulls me closer wrapping his arm around my waist before he breaks the kiss leaning his forehead on mine. "What do you need baby?"

I don't answer because I don't know what I need. He looks into my eyes, he must see his answer because he nods. "Fair enough," he takes a deep breath, pulling away from me. He keeps his hand around my waist, ◊ *maybe I can let him continue, see what happens, I've fucked different creatures before, but never a dragon.*

Getting up from the bench, I go back into the house, towards his bedroom. He doesn't follow, ◊ *I need a shower*, stripping out of my tattered dress I toss it onto the floor. Going into the bathroom, turning the shower on I hear footsteps. Not seeing him I listen, hearing the bed creak like he sat on it. Getting into the hot shower I clean myself up. When I get out I look for a towel, noticing there is one on the counter next to an oversized T-shirt with shorts. Smiling at the thoughtful act I dry off, wrapping myself with the towel before leaving the bathroom.

Zephyr hears me coming, looks up, his eyes darkening. Clearing his throat he tries to keep eye contact. "I hope you enjoyed your shower. Didn't want to wear my clothes?" he asks his voice cracking a little.

Stepping in front of him I shake my head. "I appreciate the thought Zephyr." Unwinding the towel, I let it drop to the floor watching him. His gaze follows the towel as it drops. Stepping closer, I spread my legs putting his legs between mine hovering over his lap. Running my fingers through his hair, I trail my hand to his chin, lifting it up so I can lean down kissing him softly.

His hand goes to my neck, we kiss for a few moments before he kisses my chin, down my jawbone to my neck sucking on it as he pulls me fully on his lap. Straddling his lap, wrapping my legs around his waist, I press myself closer lifting his head from my neck to continue kissing him deepening the kiss, my hands pulling his shirt up. I break from the kiss long enough to pull it off, tossing it, before returning to kiss him. He watches me intently, keeping his hands on my waist, I can feel them tense like he wants to take control but he's giving me control, he closes his eyes as we continue to make out topless together. ◊ *I could get used to this,* I say to myself, gently biting his lower lip which causes his eyes to snap open, look at me lustful, wanting. I push his chest gently making him fall back against the bed his hands on my waist, not losing eye contact.

Leaning down I kiss him deeply, my tongue gliding over his, pressing my body to his noticing a bulge in his pants. His hand traces up my body, going to my breast massaging it. Breaking from the kiss, my cheeks flushed, I push myself up a little, giving him more room.

He flips us on the bed laying me in the center, standing up but keeping my gaze as he takes his pants off. I scoot back onto the pillows of the bed, my legs spread open for him, my pussy glistening...inviting him in.

His eyes trail my body lingering at my wet pussy, lowers himself in between my legs his mouth just inches away from touching. Looking into my eyes he asks, "You want this?"

"Are you always this timid?" I ask smiling. I run my hand through his hair, gripping him gently as I pull his head between my legs to answer his question.

Chapter 5

Zephyr's POV

When Arachne pulls my head in between her legs I don't hesitate, licking between her folds. *Damn she tastes good, different then Ivy,* opening her folds for access, I circle my tongue around her clit. She moans in response when I slip a finger in her dripping pussy, pulling it in and out slowly.

Arachne seems to enjoy intimate and gentle, I think to myself as I slide my tongue into her pussy, my thumb rubbing on her clit. Swirling my tongue inside, looking for the spot to trigger a jolt through her body, I grin internally when she shudders tightening her grip in my hair.

As I rub her clit with my thumb, flicking my tongue on her g-spot, I add a second finger. Her body arches pulling my head closer, her pussy throbs as she gets close to her orgasm.

She lets out a moan as she comes apart in my mouth, her pussy clamping down on my tongue and fingers. When she rides her orgasm out I pull my tongue and fingers out, licking my lips. Starting at her thigh I kiss gingerly up her body, grinning when seeing her heated gaze. Leaning down kissing her softly, I run my hands up her body my finger's gliding like a feather. When I reach her breasts, I give them a squeeze she presses her body closer to mine. Her breath is heavy as I line myself up to her entrance keeping her gaze as I slowly push my dick into her. She moans arching her body to mine making me slide in deeper.

Kissing her neck softly I rock my hips thrusting in and out of her, keeping my stride slow and deep, *I'm going to drag this out as long as possible.* Grabbing her breast, taking one nipple into my mouth, massaging the other, keeping my slow pace her body trembling.

"Oh, Zephyr...don't stop," she's breathing heavy while she moans in pure ecstasy. "Oh, that's it." She screams out, moaning as her nails dig into my back. She's moaning so loud I'm thankful no one lives in a five mile radius. Continuing my pace I return to kissing her deeply, dominating her mouth.

The trembling increases as she gets closer to another orgasm. Feeling mine get close makes me move faster, *she's going to come undone before I do,* her eyes rolls back into her head, laying my face into the crook of her neck taking in her scent as I kiss it. Her nails dig in deeper breaking my skin, as starts to come undone under me screaming my name.

Her walls clamp down on my dick as she reaches her orgasm, making me moan. I don't stop, thrusting my hips a couple more times before coming deep inside her, breathing heavily. Feeling my dick soften I slowly pull out, rolling off her.

She's breathing heavy, her face flushed. Proud I got the job done, I smile, going to the bathroom to grab a rag. Returning with a warm washcloth I gingerly clean her up doing the same to myself. Tossing the washcloth into the hamper before I lay down on the bed next to her pulling her into my arms, her head on my chest.

She doesn't resist like I thought she would, seems to get closer instead. Within moments she drifts to sleep, smiling while gently running my fingers through her hair, I whisper, "Sleep beautiful princess, I'll be here. You are safe." She sleeps soundly, my nose nestled into the top of her head inhaling her scent helps me drift to sleep.

I wake with a start, Arachne is mumbling and whimpering in her sleep. I gently rub her shoulders trying to soothe her before she yells out, 'no, don't, please stop, I don't like that,' I whisper gently into her ears. "It's just a dream baby, you're here...with me, wake up princess."

She doesn't wake, her body tenses before shaking violently. Shaking her shoulder raising my voice a little bit I command, "Babe wake up." Still nothing. Sitting up fully I pull her into my lap gently slapping her cheek shaking her body, "Arachne, wake up. You're having a bad dream. WAKE UP!" I yell into her face, her eyes snapping open. I let out a breath I didn't realize I was holding, her eyes dart around the room quickly before settling onto my eyes.

"What happened? Everything ok?"

"I should be asking you that babe. You were stuck in a nightmare I was trying to wake you up." Her body continues shaking, I rub her back holding her close.

She nods, closing her eyes taking slow calculated breaths. "I'm ok, we get nightmares pretty frequently unfortunately." She climbs out of my arms sitting next to me, wrapping her arms around her knees pulling them to her chest like she's trying to hide herself, laying her cheek on them watching me. "Thank you for trying to wake me up."

Leaning forward I stroke her cheek giving her a smile, "of course baby, I was worried I would lose you to whatever darkness you are harboring. Would you like to tell me about it?" She shakes her head closing her eyes.

Laying back down, holding the covers inviting her back into my arms, "Let's try to get back to sleep. A good princess needs all the beauty sleep they can get." She nods, smiling slightly settling back into my arms, her arms around me snug. I run my hand down her back trying to keep her calm as she drifts back to sleep. Listening to her breath even out I sigh, *one day little mate, you will realize who I am, I hope you don't run from me. I'm never going to let you go.* I drift to sleep soundlessly holding onto my beautiful mate who doesn't even know how connected we are yet.

Arachne's POV

Slowly opening my eyes, feeling like something is weighing me down, I look around and see Zephyr's arm is draped over my stomach, his leg over mine. He's spooning me, nestled into the back of my neck breathing slow and even. Trying to gently pull his arm off me to get up when he tightens his grip.

"Go back to sleep princess. Don't you dare think about leaving me yet." He pulls me against his chest tight, trying to loosen his grip laughing a little.

"I gotta pee! Let me up Zephyr or I'll pee all over your bed," pushing against his arm, it seems like he's debating what he wants to do before he opens arm letting me go. Rushing to the bathroom shutting the door behind me I do my business. After I wash my hands I grab the clothes he had left for me last night, getting dressed, sniffing the shirt.

His scent is calming, smells like oakwood and jasmine flowers. Closing my eyes breathing it in, committing the smell to memory before going back into the bedroom. Zephyr is playing on his phone, sitting on the end of the bed, walking to him I sit on his lap smiling. "Thank you for last night, I didn't know I needed that. That was probably one of the best nights I've had in a long time."

He smiles brightly, his hand on my lower back, running his other hand on my leg, "It was definitely one of my top nights for sure. I'm glad I was able to help princess."

I give him a kiss before laying my head on his shoulder, taking a deep breath, "I need to get back to the city to deal with the aftermath of Lennix." Sighing heavily, "I don't want to go honestly. It would just cause more pain and turmoil."

Rubbing my back offering me comfort, "Then don't babe. Stay here with me, we can do whatever you want today." His voice is soft, I can tell he's sincere.

Shaking my head, looking at him, "I can't hide from my problems forever Zephyr. Also, I need to get back to my place to get blood. I'm getting hungry." Holding his gaze, I open my mouth my fangs are elongated, my gums irritated.

He turns me in his lap, facing him giving me a gentle kiss, his tongue gliding under my fangs before he whispers, "Your welcome to feed on me princess."

Pulling away, standing quickly I hold my hands up. "No, we're not allowed to feed on people. Please take me home Zeph" I plead with him crossing my arms.

He sighs in resignation, nodding as he stands, getting dressed. He holds his hand out to me, I take it he leads me to the car getting in. While we drive back to the city I look out at the rain, smiling when thunder crackles through the sky.

When we arrive at my apartment I rush inside. He's a few steps behind, opening the fridge I go rigid. Every single blood pack has been ripped open, pooling at the bottom, making it inedible. Looking around the rest of the apartment, I notice that my apartment is in disarray.

When Zeph enters the apartment he looks around cursing under his breath. "Was this Lennix?" Venom drip off his tongue as he gets angry.

I don't answer, rushing around the apartment to see the damage. My room is trashed, every mirror shattered, my bedding is shredded, when I get into the bathroom I see a pill bottle in the toilet with remnants of the potion swirling with the water. Letting out a frustrated scream I punch the wall.

Hearing me scream Zephyr comes running in freezing as he looks around me. "Arachne, we need to leave...now. Please come straight to me don't look at anything else."

My head snaps to him my eyes burning with fury, the others are fully awake in my head now. Bellatrix is trying to force control as rage increases between us, doing the opposite I turn seeing the writing on the wall.

THIS IS THE CONSEQUENCE OF DENYING ME,

it's written in blood. Starting to feel shaky I turn to Zephyr, "I think..." is all I get out before everything goes black.

🔥 Bellatrix's POV

Forcefully, I take control after seeing everything that has been done to our home. 🔥 *I'm going to fucking kill him.* Zephyr sees the change holding his hands up, almost like trying to talk down a wild animal. "Move the FUCK out of my way Zephyr." Stalking towards him slowly my fists clenched.

"I can't do that princess," he shakes his head staying in the door frame. "Don't rush headfirst, let me help you please."

Shaking my head I push past him, I push him a little too hard making him fly across the room slamming against a wall collapsing on the floor. "Stay out of my way, don't make me hurt you." Storming out of the apartment I jog towards the wolf settlement.

I'm jogging through the woods silently, fury boiling in my blood when wings flapping can be heard as a giant red dragon slams into a clearing blocking my path, staring at my direction. Stopping in front of him, slightly out of breath, I stare back. My shoulders are rising, my body trembling as the rage in me starts to reach dangerous levels.

Zephyr shifts standing before me naked, "Bellatrix calm down, you're not thinking straight! You don't want to storm in there and start a war."

"I'll burn this world to the ground if it means he is in ashes. He violated our safe space! He's violated our body! He deserves everything I give him and more!" I get up in his face shoving his chest hard, but he doesn't budge or back up.

He grabs my arms, pinning them to my sides hard, "Baby girl...I agree with you. But there is a way to hurt him without causing a war. Calm the fuck down!"

Narrowing my eyes at his tone I headbutt him hard in the face, making him stagger back releasing my arms, hitting him with a right hook, but he dodges easily grabbing my wrist, twisting it behind my back snagging my left arm, pinning it there as well. I'm breathing heavy, he wraps an arm around my chest, pinning me tight against his body.

"Calm the fuck down." His head snaps up, he lets out a growl, "We need to go. Now!" he picks me up, carrying me over his shoulder like a ragdoll as he starts to run. Howls are heard before we can get out of the clearing, when about 20 wolves of various sizes begin circling us. Zephyr curses setting me down on my feet, holding onto me tightly.

A giant black wolf starts trotting towards us. It drops a robe it was carrying in its maw before it shifts, Lennix stands covering himself up with the robe with a grin. "Well, what do we have here?" He walks towards us, I struggle in Zephyr's hold trying to break out so I can pound his smug face in. "Thank you for bringing my fiancé back, I've been worried about her. I heard her place got trashed, we have been hunting for her."

Zephyr tenses but he stays still and quiet, keeping his hold on me firm. I break the silence, "Hunting is definitely the right word however you have it backwards I'm hunting you." The other wolves growl and snarl at me, Lennix grins wider, amused.

"Oh Hunny, your delusions are dangerous. You should come and let my pack doctor check you out. You seem to be having a mental breakdown." He starts walking towards us, every step he takes Zephyr takes one backwards pulling me with him.

"You're not putting a finger on her," Zephyr says, swooping me into his arms cradling my body close. "Hold on tight baby," he whispers just loud enough for me to hear.

He shifts and because of how his hands were around me, his dragon form appears with me clinging onto his neck. Scrambling myself to sit, my legs behind his wing joint, he lets out a deafening roar. My hands start to get really hot around his throat as he prepares to blow fire into the clearing.

The wolves have already started to scatter, Lennix stares up at me with hatred and disbelief. He sees embers starting to ignite in Zephyr's maw, shifting to run off before the fire sprays all over the grass.

Zephyr takes off in a ring of fire flying through the air. It takes everything I have to hold on, so I don't fling off his body. We fly for a while going towards the mountains, he lands at the river by his house, leaning down so I can slide off. He shifts, not saying a word as he walks towards the house shoving the door open.

He left me standing by the river in silence. I stare at the river, my heart pounding but I feel the rage slowly simmering down. *who the fuck does Zephyr think he is to interfere?* I ask the others.

Lilli speaks first, *He was trying to stop you from getting killed. Lennix was ready for you Trix. You would've started a war.* She goes silent, I feel when she closes herself off.

I was doing what needed to be done, he deserves to die. He has raped, beaten, degraded, and humiliated us for years. I'm done letting him get away with it. I tell the others grabbing a rock from the bed of the river, throwing it hard at the forest. It whistles loudly through the air making a loud crack when it strikes the tree.

Arachne pulls at the door silently asking to regain control, I don't want to give it up yet, sighing I close my eyes letting her take over.

Chapter 6

◊ *Arachne's POV*

Opening my eyes, watching the flow of the river for a little longer before turning towards Zephyr's house. Seeing him standing at the door, arms crossed watching me, I sigh heavily, heading towards him.

Stopping in front of him, "Thank you for bringing us here, for keeping her from making a mistake." Looking in his eyes which are narrowed and pissed off, I shrink a little, "I need to go clean my apartment and contact my parents. Would you like to join me?"

He stares at me for a bit before lowering his arms nodding. He grabs the keys to his Jetta, "Let's go. I don't want to take too long."

Following him to the car I get in quietly, he drives us back to the city. After a while he breaks the silence, "I won't be welcome at your parents, they would know what I am...I don't want you to go in alone."

I grab my phone from my pocket, "I won't be alone, I'll call a friend, he is my Shadow after all." He gives a small "hmm," as I pull up my contact list and find Lucas' name, hitting call putting the phone to my ear. It didn't even ring once before he answered.

"Hey sweetheart, I've missed you." I can hear the roar of his bike, making me shake my head.

"Pull over Lucas," I tell him in a curt tone not giving room for argument. I'm the only one that calls him his birth name all the time...the others call him that when he needs to be serious.

I hear the tires screech on the other end of the phone, the engine turned off immediately after.
"Arachne...something's wrong, this isn't a social call is it?"

Sighing heavily, I look at Zephyr driving, "No, I need your help. Meet me at my place in 20 minutes. Please bring a blood bag for me."

"You got it." He hangs up.

I put my phone back in my pocket, reaching to hold Zephyr's hand. He allows me to take it, I pull it into my lap gently rubbing it, closing my eyes at the warmth radiating from him. "My friend will meet us at the apartment, don't kill him please? No harm will come from him."

He nods, rubbing his thumb along my hand in silent support. We pull up to my place, I see a motorcycle parked in front of it. Slapping my palm to my face when noticing he changed the paint job. It's black with neon orange stripes and a purple silhouette of a wolf, it sticks out like a sore thumb around here.

Zephyr looks around, wondering what I'm seeing before giving an amused laugh, "That's an interesting paint job...wonder who that belongs to?"

"An idiot who loves to stand out when he can blend in better." I get out of the car, going into my apartment. I barely get in the door before I'm swept off my feet in a bear hug. Zephyr tries to push into the room to pull me away when I swat at his hands. "He isn't hurting me, let me down you big oaf!" Laughing genuinely as Lucas lowers me down to my feet.

"I came in to sit down, found the place trashed...I got worried about you." He checks me over, brushing my hair out of my face to look me in the eyes. He searches my eyes for something before shaking his head, backing away. He goes into the kitchen, "I'm warming up blood for you, hope you don't mind?"

Walking inside I take in the damage sighing, "I don't mind, thank you Lucas." He growls when I use his name, I just roll my eyes. "you've known me a long time, I won't use your dumb ass nickname that Bellatrix gave you."

Zephyr looks at me curiously, cleaning the chairs and couch off so we can sit down. He takes the couch with his arm out expecting me to sit with him. Shaking my head I sit in my favorite chair by the window sitting on my legs. "Lucas is my childhood best friend, we know each other better than anyone. He was exiled by my parent's when he turned 13."

Lucas sits in the chair across from me with a sad smile after handing me a glass with blood in it, "I had to learn everything on my own. It broke my heart the day I had to leave."

Zephyr looks at Lucas, assessing him, I'm sure he's trying to get a read on him. Lucas notices, nudging his head toward him, "who's the dude sweetheart?"

Zephyr's eyes narrow at the nickname he has for me I raise my eyebrow at him, "This is a friend of ours, his name is Zephyr. He knows about us he helped stop Trix from starting a war." I look at Lucas, smiling, "You look good Lucas, life as a nomad is doing you good." I look him over and damn.... he's not the scrappy kid I knew before. He's taller, his Latino heritage giving him a nice coppery color, his muscles bulging from his shirt, his hair has a messy look to it like it was deliberate. His eyes are golden brown with a red ring around them, symbolic to the vampire blood running through him.

He shoots me a dazzling smile, "It's been a fun adventure, but I still want to settle down and be home. I think I finally found where that's supposed to be." I look at him confused then at Zephyr who shrugs clearing his throat.

"We should get back on topic, this place isn't safe for Lilliana or the others, Arachne says she needs to speak to her parents. The reason you are here is to go with her. Think you can manage that and not allow her to get hurt?" he leans forward his hands folded on his knees watching Lucas curiously.

Lucas' face snaps to Zephyr he growls, "I'm more than capable, but you are an idiot if you can't see she can protect herself." They both stand quickly, Lucas is ready to lunge at Zephyr when I jump in between them my hand on both of their chests.

"Don't even think about it Lucas Bane. I'll not tolerate violence towards my friends." I look him in the eyes before looking at Zephyr, "you also need to knock off your shit. Don't antagonize him." Taking a deep breath, turning towards Lucas. "Will you please go with to my parents? I don't want to go alone, Lennix attacked me and is using my parents as leverage to keep me under his thumb."

Lucas looks down at me his eyes softening, "I'll go wherever you need me to sweetheart, I don't care if it's the lion's den or the pits of the underworld. You need me...I'm there. That's all there is to it."

"Let's get going. Zephyr will you stay and clean this up for me please? We will be back to help as soon as possible." He gives me a nod, I take Lucas' hand, he tenses at my touch before gripping my hand gently but firmly. Looking at Zephyr and he tosses me a set of keys.

I catch them looking at him curiously, "Take the Jetta, I left it behind when I went to find Bellatrix after she ran off so it's still outside." He smiles, "Don't let the big guy crash it."

I laugh, "He's not driving. Thank you, see you soon." The two of us head outside, I go towards the black Jetta on the road getting in the driver's side. Lucas climbs into the passenger side looking over at me.

"You know...if you did what I think you did they won't tolerate the disrespect. They also won't tolerate you bringing me back." He grabs my hand firmly folding his fingers in mine.

Nodding I give his hand a squeeze, "That's why I need my favorite Lucas to get me out if they try to keep me there. I know I can count on you Lucas...you've never let me down before."

"I never will sweetheart, I'll be by your side till the end of time." He smiles warmly. I drive us towards the center of the city where the vampire coven made their base. It's an old Victorian style hotel that has been modernized to keep with the times but still kept the old style.

I park the car a block away getting out, staring at the hotel. "Better get it over with," Getting to the sidewalk I wait for Lucas, he comes up next to me taking my hand. I lock the car, we walk to the hotel, getting through the revolving doors before I'm stopped by security.

"Princess Lilliana, come with us, your father wishes to speak to you." They grab my arm trying to pull me away from Lucas.

I struggle against their hold, grabbing their wrist tight, "Don't separate us, he comes with me!" Lucas tries to push past the guards separating us.

The guard looks at him shaking his head. "He isn't welcome here, He can either wait in the lobby quietly or be thrown out on the street like the trash he is." He looks at Lucas with disgust as he pulls me forcefully towards the elevator.

I look at Lucas frowning, "It'll be ok Lucas, I won't be far, I'll stick to the darkness."

He looks at me understanding what I was saying, he shoves the guard off him going outside. The guard lead me into the elevator, I cross my arms holding them close. The doors open to the penthouse, I see my father standing by the window his back to me as he looks out at the city. The guard pulls me in, pushing me to the couch.

"Stop manhandling me asshole." I spit out shoving his arm off me making my father turn looking at me with his brown eyes, the red rings glowing faintly in the dimly lit room.

"Leave us Grigorio," he orders the guard. Grigorio gives him a bow going back into the elevator. My father walks toward me sitting in the chair across from me. "Lilliana my dear, you look worse for wear. When are you going to come home?" He asks with a faint tone of condescension. My parents hate the fact I want to live somewhere out of their control.

I shake my head, "Never, I don't want to live here where I'm caged all the time. I don't want to be a puppet." My body is shaking, I hate how nervous my father makes me.

He clears his throat making my gaze snap to his, "You are my heir. It's your duty to lead our people, to make us reach the top of this world. I've allowed you to indulge in your whims. Now it's time to be who you were born to be."

Shooting to my feet I argue back, "I will not! You didn't allow me to do anything! I ran away! You don't control me father. I'll be my own person, make my own choices. One of them being I won't marry Lennix Wolfe."

His eyes flare in pure anger as he watches me, "Yes you will, you will marry that dog and unite our kinds under one rule. You will be Queen of the vampires AND Luna of the wolf kingdom. This is your birthright."

"I will not!! I would rather die than be tied to that fool. He is an abusive manipulating bastard that deserves more than death." I walk towards the wall getting away from him, I feel a slight tug on my finger from the shadows, taking a deep breath calming myself.

My father stands, taking a step towards me, "If you deny this, then I won't help you any longer. You will be alone, not a part of this family any longer. Don't be a stupid petulant girl."

I give a dry laugh shaking my head, "You don't know me at all father, I'm never alone. Goodbye." When I say those words he sees a shimmer in the shadow trying to grab me before I disappear into the darkness.

When I materialize I'm beside the Jetta with Lucas holding my hand, he pulls me into a hug keeping me there while I wait for my senses to return. "Thank you Lucas, I appreciate that." I unlock the car, we get in driving back to my apartment.

While driving I notice a couple of cars in my mirror, "Looks like my father can't take a hint. We are being followed." I pull into the driveway getting inside quickly. "We need Bellatrix, if this comes to a fight she's the only one worth a damn," I tell Lucas as we get into the door and I slam it behind both of us.

Zephyr comes out of the bedroom drying his hands and sees me slamming the door. "What's going on babe?" Zephyr tosses the towel, walks over to me taking my face into his hands looking in my eyes. "What happened?"

Lucas takes off his shirt, tosses it onto the counter backing up as he shifts into his hybrid form. His eyes turned a darker shade of brown the red showing brighter, he has black fur all over, his mouth showing his fangs fully extended, his hand thickening as his nails turn to sharp claws, his voice deeper as he talks, "Her father is trying to force her into a life of servitude. She denied him so he followed us back. He plans to take her by force."

I look at Zephyr who has a dark look in his eyes, giving a crooked smile, "I need Bellatrix for this, he won't stop. If I run he will just follow. It's time to let her do what she does best...she won't let them take us alive."

He frowns, "That's my fear. I would rather you be alive, but if fighting is what needs to happen then we will fight. Just tell her to fight smarter not harder. Stay alive." He leans down giving me a soft kiss before pulling me into my chair. "We will give you a few minutes to switch," he sniffs the air, "you have 5 before they get here."

"That's all we need," I close my eyes reaching into our mindscape, kicking the door open.

⬭ Mindscape

⬭ "Girls we've got a problem, Father is chasing us and has us cornered in our apartment." I yell out, heading towards my door.

Lilliana blanches, looks at me then Ivy and Bellatrix. "What do we do? I can't go back there."

"We won't and he is going to learn the hard way how to take a hint." Bellatrix's eyes are a raging inferno, I look at her pointing to the door. She nods understanding, the rest of us rush into our rooms shutting the doors tight where we are completely blocked off, she needs 100% focus right now. "Oh, I'm going to enjoy this." Bellatrix says as she walks through the door pulling it shut completely behind her.

Chapter 7

 *Bellatrix's POV*

I open my eyes, Zephyr and Lucas watching me. I give Lucas a sly smile standing up, "Time to kick some ass my friend." Running into my bedroom, change into shorts and a form fitting tank top, put on my black combat boots, I open a paneling in the floorboard and pull out the wooden box. I gently brush my hand over the inscription, before opening it seeing 12 beautiful black daggers with a black leather handle, small rubies adorning the hilt. I put my harness on sheathing the daggers heading back to the guys.

They both give me a heated look as they look me over before they look at each other. Zephyr speaks first, "They don't know what they are walking into."

Lucas gives him a playful nudge in his shoulder, "Nope, she's deadly without the daggers, with them...she's a walking grim reaper." His eyes are trailing down my body making me roll my eyes. I hear car doors open outside the apartment as both guys turn to face the front door.

Within moments chaos erupts. The front door bursts open as 2 of the vampire guards storm in, rushing towards the guys. The window shatters as 2 more jump through heading towards me. "You should not have done that," I say to the 2 that broke my window, grabbing a dagger firmly in my hand before rushing towards them slicing one in the throat causing him to fall to his knees, stabbing the other in his chest leaving my dagger embedded in his heart. I grab the guy who fell by his neck digging my fingers into the cut, pulling at his head, I begin to hear a rip. I snarl, pulling with more force making his head rip off. I drop his head to the floor kicking his body beside it.

The guys are fighting with the first 2 vampire guards but seem to be struggling. One has their arms around Zephyr's throat, lean down to bite into him. I don't think...I rush, throwing a dagger right between his eyes with so much force he is thrown back yanking Zephyr with him. I jump over the couch, drop kicking the guy fighting with Lucas against the wall. Lucas reaches forward plunging his now clawed hand into the guards chest ripping out his heart.

More guards rush in, I throw daggers aiming for their hearts as they come through the door hitting them square where I want to. After the last one falls dead in the hallway I hear a car door close, tires screech off into the distance.

Turning to Zephyr and Lucas, my eyes red and gold instead of Lilli's usual green and red. Lucas looks at me unafraid, Zephyr looks at me with heat in his own. "We need to get out of here, let's get to my place." He looks at Lucas, "think you can use your trick to get us there?"

Lucas nods then looks at me. "Whenever your ready sweetheart, let's get goin'."

Nodding I look around at the apartment, gathering all of the daggers I used, sheathing them. I go into the bedroom grabbing a duffle bag throwing clothes as well as any other things we might need. I toss it towards the bedroom door before looking at the panel on the floor. *We aren't getting our deposit back...sorry Lilli.* I smash my foot into a few other panels making a big hole, pulling out a wooden chest. "Hey Shadow, can you give me a hand please?"

Lucas comes in, his mouth drops in shock at the giant box in front of me, "where the fuck..." his eyes droop to the giant hole in the floor then laughs, "Ahh you're a clever little devil aren't you. Soo many secrets you guys carry."

"Shut up and help me," I pull the duffle bag over my shoulder and grab one end, he grabs the other. We go back to the living room. "Change of plans Zeph, we are driving. This will fit in the backseat just fine, I call the Jetta," He looks at me in surprise then nods heading outside.

We get everything loaded up, driving in separate vehicles. Zephyr is in the black Charger, I'm in the Jetta, and Lucas is riding on his bike. We fly through traffic, arriving at Zephyr's place quickly. I park next to him, grab the box pulling it out, when it hits the gravel it makes a loud thud. Lucas grabs the other end taking it inside with me.

I drop the box at the end of the stairs, looking at Zephyr. "I'm going to need a place to put this that's hard to access or find. When the time comes, you'll know more about it."

He gives me a nod, "Give me some time I will have that for you. First thing first, what can we do to extinguish the anger in your eyes princess?"

Shrugging I look to both of them, "You tell me. I usually need to beat someone to a pulp a couple times to get my aggression out. I highly doubt you want me to kick your asses"

I shrug out of my harness, unsheathe my daggers placing them back into the wooden box that I stuffed in my duffle bag, take off my boots setting them by the door. When I stand up Zephyr steps in front of me. I raise my eyes at him, "there's something called personal space...maybe you've heard of it?"

He laughs like I just made a joke before grabbing me roughly by the hair, slamming his mouth to mine. I barely had time to react, I push against his chest when suddenly I have another mouth on the back of my neck pushing me firm against Zephyr as Lucas bites my neck scraping against the skin.

A moan escapes my mouth, Zephyr uses the opening to shove his tongue into my mouth dominating mine. He kisses me deeply biting my lip when I try to pull away. Lucas' hand slides up my shirt gripping my breasts hard.

Zephyr breaks from the kiss and there's heat in his eyes like he can't get enough. My breath is heavy. "Fuck it," I grab his shirt by the collar, ripping his shirt down the middle, pulling him back down to my mouth kissing him deep. Lucas grabs my shirt from the hem and pulls it upwards.

"Stop kissing him." Lucas orders me, his voice deeper. Breaking from the kiss Lucas spins me facing him pulling my shirt off my head tossing it onto the floor. "My turn," he kisses me rough, *my lips are going to be bruised for sure after all of this.*

I hear Zephyr moving around before he comes back, grabs my wrists pulling them to my back. "Do you trust us?" he asks, Lucas breaks from the kiss long enough for me to answer.

"Yes," I reply breathlessly. He looks at Lucas and nods. Lucas grabs me by the throat kissing me again. I can feel rope start to wrap around my wrists. 🔥 *Ohhh fuck...this is going to be fun.* After my wrists are secure Lucas lifts me by my hips, carries me to the bedroom tossing me onto the bed. I look up at Zephyr and Lucas wondering what they are doing.

Zephyr grins tossing the ripped shirt onto the floor, undoing his pants letting them drop his erection springs free, he yanks mine off. He grabs me by my ankles, flips me over so I'm face first on the bed. He pulls one ankle to the corner, I feel a rope securing me there then he does the same to the other.

I look over my shoulder, Lucas is undressing himself, the two men couldn't be more different for dick size, but both don't seem to care. Zephyr is long with decent girth, but Lucas is thick and probably 2 inches shorter than Zephyr. 🔥 *Delicious*...I bite my lip watching them, Lucas smacks my ass, I jolt a little biting back a moan as it left a nice sting.

"You're not allowed to bite your lip sweetheart. That's our job." To make a point he bites my ass cheek making my pussy wetter. Lucas runs a hand up the back of my body till he gets to my hair. Fisting it tight, he pulls my head up arching my neck, slams his mouth to mine kissing me roughly.

Zephyr grabs my arms still bound to my back, pulling me up onto my knees yanking me from the kiss with Lucas, my back flush against his. "Don't move." He orders me as he loosens the rope on my arm, he leaves one wrist tied, ties it to a hook in the ceiling. He grabs another rope doing the same to the other arm. I keep my eyes on Lucas the whole time, I didn't think it was possible, but I could swear his dick was getting harder.

Lucas gets on the bed in front of me, also on his knees kissing my breasts one by one, being gentle at first before he starts biting and pulling at my nipple. He grabs my breasts massaging them with every bite and kiss.

I lay my head back breathing heavy still against Zephyr's chest who leans down kissing and sucking on my neck. Zephyr runs a hand down my stomach, slipping a finger in between the folds of my pussy. He gives my neck a bite before slipping a finger inside. I give an appreciative moan trying to grind against his hand, but he has me firm against him.

Lucas notices what I was trying to do and laughs, "no sweetheart, you don't get to run the show today." He runs his hands down my body till they get to my hips, and he slides them behind me gripping my ass. Zephyr moves his hand away backing away from me. Lucas lifts me from my ass as Zephyr grabs my ankles standing me up, my arms still hooked on the ceiling.

Zephyr nods to Lucas, he pushes my back to where I'm now bent over in Lucas's lap, but my ass is sticking in perfect line for Zephyr's dick. Zephyr gets on his knees, devouring my pussy like it's his last meal, his finger rubbing my clit hard. Lucas wastes no time after Zephyr eats me out, grabbing my hair moving it out of my face sliding his dick in my mouth. I close my eyes moaning onto his dick as he fucks my mouth hard and fast.

My body starts to shake while Zephyr continues eating me out, my orgasm getting closer with each touch and lick. He slid 2 fingers inside moving them around in tune with his tongue.

Lucas hasn't let up, still fucking my mouth, drool leaking out the side as I moan onto his dick making it vibrate on my tongue. He grips my hair tighter, I can feel his dick tense as he's getting close.

When an orgasm rips through me making my eyes roll back to my head, Lucas slams his dick in my throat with a guttural groan shooting his load. I swallow it all up, licking it as he pulls himself away panting.

He is still sporting a hard on, my body feels weak, but I'm not done, I need more. Arching my body pulling myself up by the ropes, so I can see Lucas face to face. "Sure, hope you're not done yet, cuz I sure as fuck ain't."

Lucas grins shaking his head, "Fuck no, I'm just getting started. By the time this is over you will be so full it's going to show for days." My body shivers in anticipation at his words.

"Prove it," is all I manage to get out before he kisses my mouth roughly while Zephyr is moving to the side of the bed.

Lucas slides off the bed between my legs sitting on the floor, my pussy right at his mouth. Zephyr pulls me down by my throat and kisses me deeply as he sits in front of me, he pulls my head towards his dick moving my hair out of my face. "Get to work princess, show me what that mouth can do."

Taking it like a challenge, I take him into my mouth as far as I can choking a little bit, *I still haven't gotten to his base*. Lucas licks my clit sliding a finger in my pussy which is still dripping from my previous orgasm. I bob my head up and down taking Zephyr's dick deeper with each movement.

Lucas circles his finger around sliding in 2 more. I moan onto Zeph's dick, he tightens his hold on my hair now moving my head at a pace he wants. Lucas pumps his fingers in and out, swirling his tongue around my clit. My body starts to tremble as another orgasm threatens to rip through me.

Lucas feels me tremble, pumps his fingers faster, swirling his tongue slower. My moan is muffled by Zephyr's dick as I come all over Lucas' fingers, Zephyr loses his control and spills out in the back of my throat, his hands in my hair keeping me there making sure I get everything.

Zephyr pulls me by my hair, leaning down giving me a deep kiss tasting himself and Lucas mixed together in my mouth. He undoes the ropes on my wrist, "untie her ankles." He tells Lucas while he slides himself back onto the bed further.

Lucas does what he says, when my ankles are free I crawl onto Zephyr straddling him, his dick just brushing my entrance. He puts his hands on my waist before slamming me down onto him, I arch my back moaning. Lucas watches us, slowly rubbing his dick, "where do you keep your lube Zephyr?" he asks.

Zephyr points to the table by the bed and Lucas moves to it, finds the lube, rubs it over his dick moving onto the bed behind me. "Bend over. I would hold onto the pillow by his head sweetheart." I do as he says, looking at Zephyr's face as he is still fully seated in my pussy. I give him a deep heated kiss, which he returns without hesitation. Lucas presses into my ass with his dick, after a moment he slams deep inside.

I give out a pained moan, he stops letting me adjust. *These guys are going to ruin our body.* I nod my head keeping Zephyr's gaze, he grins back to Lucas, "The greedy girl is ready."

That was all Lucas needed before he started moving himself in and out. He started slow getting into a rhythm before speeding up and going harder my body bouncing off of Zephyr's dick. Zephyr holds onto my hips keeping me in place as he starts moving his hips rocking his dick in and out at the same pace Lucas goes.

The house echoes with my moaning as I get louder screaming their names. Lucas bites along my back kissing it, Zephyr does the same along the front, both of them not slowing down. My body arches as a 3rd orgasm rips through. I'm screaming their name as loud as possible. Zephyr buries himself deep inside me shooting his load, Lucas pumps a couple times before slamming himself deep, shooting his own. He collapses onto of me pressing me against Zephyr's chest, all 3 of us breathing heavily.

Lucas pulls himself out of me with a groan, walks to the bathroom turning on the water. He comes out a few seconds later with 2 warm rags handing one to Zephyr. He uses one to wipe between my legs cleaning me up then cleans himself up tossing it onto the floor before collapsing onto the bed.

Zephyr pulls himself out, cleans up the little mess he makes before cleaning himself up. "Well...that gives a whole new definition to hot and heavy." He strokes my hair helping me down into the bed, covering me up with a blanket kissing my head, "Sleep princess, we will be here when you wake up."

I curl into Lucas' side closing my eyes, I inhale his scent, he smells like chocolate with mint, I begin to drift away feeling safe.

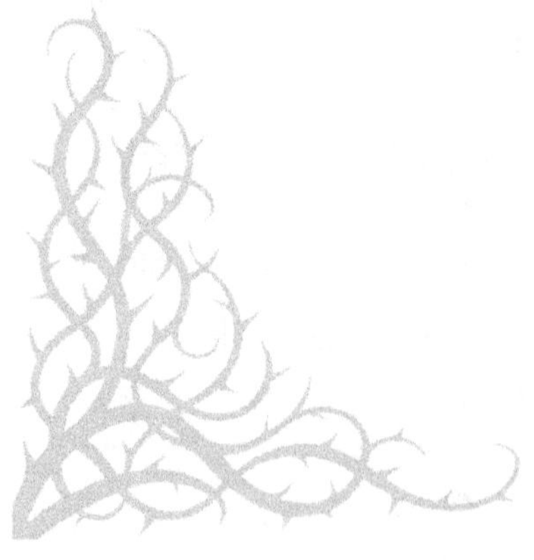

Chapter 8

Lucas' POV

I watch Bellatrix fall into a deep sleep before looking at Zephyr on the other side. He's watching her like she's the world to him, sighing as I carefully pull myself from under her. She doesn't move, I pull my pants back on pointing to the deck, motioning for Zephyr to follow.

Nodding he gets up, pulls some shorts on, tucking Bellatrix in and giving a light kiss to her head trying not to disturb her. He opens the door sitting in one of the chairs leaning back looking at the night sky.

I sit across from him, pull out a pack of cigarettes from my pocket lighting one up taking a long drag from it. I offer the pack to him, "Want a smoke?"

"Nah, I'm good, thanks though. I quit years ago, I don't wanna start up again." He smiles while taking a deep breath.

"Alright man," I take a few drags looking at the mountains hearing the river before I turn towards him. "Why are you so enamored with my mate? Are you the reason she can't feel the bond with me?"

He looks at me confused shaking his head, "Your mate?"

I flick the finished cigarette into the grass after smothering the lit part into the concrete. "Yeah, I just found out when I got back today... when I hugged her. I was hoping she'd feel it too, but she didn't react...I hadn't seen her since my first shift, so I never felt it before."

"She's my mate too…I've known for a few days now." He says with a heavy sigh running his hand through his hair, "she didn't recognize me either."

"How is that possible?" Looking at him, leaning forward, "how can she have 2 mates AND how can she not know we are her mates?"

He shrugs, "I honestly don't know, having multiple mates is unheard of. It's almost impossible to block the mate bond too, only a powerful magic user can do it."

I lean back against my chair frowning, "What do we do?"

"We stick around, help her through whatever life throws at her. We don't give up on her or leave. And we look into what could've happened to cause someone to curse her." Zephyr gets up, walking to the edge of the deck leaning against the post. "There is also the issue about Lennix and her parents. What can you tell me about them?"

Laughing dryly, "Alpha Lennix is a grade A prick, which is putting it nicely. He is next in line for the Alpha King. The Nightshade Coven is the biggest coven in the world and have always been greedy for power. The Wolfe family have also been greedy, trying to grow their kingdom in order to rival any other Coven or Kingdom. They relish in control, the Nightshade's relish in dominance. Queen Amelia only had 1 child in the last 700 years, King Julian has tried to impregnate other females, but each one would be stillborn. All they had was Lilliana, their 'evil one', so they tried to marry her off to Lennix as a way to bring the 2 kingdoms together, their ultimate goal is to overthrow the Wolfe family."

Zephyr turns to me confused, "Evil one? How was Lilliana an evil child at birth?"

I get up, leaning on the other post, "She was born on a blood moon...the first vampire child to be born under one in hundreds of years. It's rumored that the gods gave her a curse as a result and that's why she has her eyes. One blood eye of the evil vampire she is one green eye of the innocence she never will be." Looking up at the half-moon, the sky is dark, but I can still see the stars from here. "I don't believe in that, I think the gods blessed her. She is stronger than she would let anyone else see, has compassion, which is rare in our world, and she has gifts I've never seen."

"What do you mean?" he asks looking at the moon.

I consider the best way to answer, "you know how some witches can see a person's aura? The color their soul gives off to know their moods or purity they have?" he nods so I continue, "She can see more than that, she can see the color of someone's magic, she can track their scent for hundreds of miles regardless if you cover it up later. Once she has your scent, she will never lose sight of where you are again."

Zeph looks down before turning to face me entirely, "why can't she feed on a live body? Her first night staying with me she told me she needed to get her blood bag because she was hungry, I offered her to feed on me, but she almost bolted at the thought. She said she is forbidden from biting a live person regardless of race."

I let out a sigh, "It's something her parents told her as a child, I offered the same once. She reacted the same way. Apparently if she bites a person they die a horrible agonizing death." I look at him, my face hardens, "I'm pretty sure it's bullshit too, every other vampire or hybrid is allowed to feed, yet the vampire princess isn't? It makes no sense."

"Another thing to investigate," Zephyr says. We hear whimpering, both of our heads snap to the door seeing Bellatrix clinging onto the sheets whining, "table this for now, let's go calm her down." He says as he opens the door, gets back in bed laying down facing her stroking her hair gently, she starts to calm to his touch.

I feel a slight pang of jealousy as she reacts to him, crawling into bed behind her wrapping my arm around her waist I pull her to my chest. She calms completely going back to a restless sleep. "We should get some sleep, we can deal with the rest later." I tell Zephyr snuggling into the back of Bellatrix's hair inhaling her scent calming my wolf.

He nods, puts his arm around hers stroking her back, lays his head down with his forehead touching hers, it doesn't take long before I hear his breathing even. I don't take long to follow drifting to a dreamless sleep.

Dream State

Opening my eyes I see it's bright as shit. I blink a couple times to get accustomed to it, looking around, I'm in a beautiful meadow surrounded by flowers. I see a pathway and begin to walk down it, my hands brushing against the flowers as I walk. Looking around I don't see anyone, *where am I?* I call out hoping to connect to the other girls. Not getting a response I continue walking enjoying the beauty. A bright light covers the area blinding me, when I open them again the meadow is on fire.

"No!" I yell at the top of my lungs, 🔥 *it's a dream...I can control this.* I try to control the fire bringing into my body. The flames flicker growing more intense at my attempt to control it, "STOP!!" I yell the flames suddenly freezing in place. I hold my hands out palms facing the flames, "VANISH!" the flames slowly go into my palms, they don't burn, I look at the charred wasteland dropping to my knees.

"You can't always save everything from damage dear," a voice calls out, I look up but can't see anyone. I stand following where I heard the voice emanating from.

Coming across a lake I see a woman by the water, her back towards me. I walk toward her cautiously, "who are you?"

"The question isn't who I'm, but who are you child?" She turns towards me, my breath catches. She's the most beautiful creature I've ever laid eyes on.

"I'm princess Lilliana Nightshade." I give the safe answer because I don't know this woman. Giving the wrong people information about us could be deadly.

The lady gives a laugh that's very melodic, "Try again Bellatrix. I already know who you are, it would be wise not to try to lie to me."

I frown, "If you know me, why did you ask?"

"Because I wanted to see how you would answer. Would you forsake your vow to your sisters, or would you honor it? I'm pleased that you chose to honor it, others say you wouldn't." She smiles at me holding out a hand, "walk with me, I would like to have a talk with you."

I look at her hand warily before taking it, we walk down the beach, the moon shining brightly. "Who are you? Where are we?"

She considers my questions walking slow, "We are in the ether, think of it like Limbo for other super-naturals of your world. This is where the animal sides of others go when they are not out in the human world, it's a peaceful realm to keep them safe." She lets me process before speaking some more, "As for who I am, my name is Selene. This is my domain, I'm the goddess of all supernatural creatures."

I freeze in my steps looking at her shocked, "What? Why would you come to me? I'm not special."

"On the contrary child, you are more special than you realize. You and the others have gifts. When Lilliana was born I came to her, I gave her the gift of sight and the gift to have multiple souls. I also put the rest of you inside her deliberately." She turns towards me holding my hand, her face slowly turning into a frown, "I was hoping you 3 girls would be dormant longer until you were ready, but I could not have foreseen what Lilliana went through. I'm deeply sorry for the pain you've suffered."

She looks out at the lake then back to me, "Evil is moving against you girls, I'm here to warn you. Trust in your instincts, they won't lead you astray. Don't be afraid of the magic inside of you. While you may see it as destruction, the others can help turn it into beauty. Help them grow their powers while you grow your own."

Sighing she strokes my cheek, "You have grown to be a marvelous creature, don't ever forget you have been blessed by me at birth. I love you...my beautiful daughter." She vanishes in the blink of an eye.

I look out at the lake, closing my eyes and taking deep breaths. I feel the wind blow against my face, it should be cool but it's warm and inviting. I feel peaceful, I open my eyes watching the lake sitting down on the beach.

Before long I'm woken up in the physical world, my body being shaken. When I open my eyes I see 2 sets of eyes staring at me in worry. Blinking to clear the haze from the dream I see Zephyr and Lucas hovering over me clearly making me laugh, "What's wrong?"

Lucas touches my face before relaxing, "You were burning up. We were trying to wake you up, but you weren't responding...we were worried about you."

I push myself up, sitting, stretching, "I feel fine, great actually," Zephyr sits beside me putting the back of his hand against my forehead.

Pushing his hand away gently laughing, "Really, I do. That was the best night sleep I've had in I don't know how long."

Zephyr clears his throat nodding, "I'm going to get started on breakfast, anything particular this princess wants?" He asks as he stands.

I think about it for a moment before giving him a grin, "Waffles...with sausage and bacon." Lucas laughs hugging me close to him.

Zephyr smiles, "Anything for my beautiful princess." He kisses my head before leaving the room, I hear clattering in the kitchen.

Lucas looks at me holding a hand out, "Wanna lay down while we wait or take a bath sweetheart?"

I roll my eyes, "Bath will win every time." Getting out of the bed I look in my duffle bag for clothes while Lucas goes and starts the bath.

When I walk in, he's waiting by the bathtub, hand out stretched with a grin "Ladies first."

I take his hand stepping into the bath shuddering at the heat, as I lower myself down he climbs in behind me sitting comfortably. I lean myself back against his chest closing my eyes relaxing in the warmth. "Just like old times huh?" I ask keeping my eyes closed.

"No, it'll be different this time, I won't be leaving again." He wraps his arms around me holding me close against him. He keeps us like that for a while before he gently pushes me off his chest, grabs a little cup off the side of the bath and runs water through my hair.

He washes my hair being gentle, avoiding soap into my eyes. After he rinses my hair he grabs a sponge, slowly washing my body, I relax at his touch. As his hands trail further down my stomach my legs open inviting him in.

He breathes onto my neck before giving it a gentle kiss, tosses the sponge to the side of the bath putting his hands back between my legs. He slides a finger in my folds brushing against my clit, his other hand caressing my breast. I slide one hand behind my back stroking his erection.

"Sweetheart, you're going to be the death of me," he whispers against my throat as he kisses and sucks on the tender skin. He slips a finger into my pussy rubbing my clit with his thumb.

I lean against his hand lifting my hips to give him better access, biting my lip. My hand still stroking him up and down, "I need you inside me. Please Shadow..." That was all he needed before he removed his hand from between my legs, unclogs the bath turning me around so I'm straddling him.

I wrap my legs behind his back and slide myself onto his dick slowly. He leans backwards a little, so I take him all the way down to his base. His hands roam up to my breasts massaging them as I move myself up and down his shaft. He moves his hips in tune with mine, thrusting harder as I come down. I arch my back moaning, he takes one hand off my breast sliding it between us rubbing my clit in circles.

My body responds to his touch, leaning into him, moving faster, "Oh Shadow, more, harder" I moan out. He grasps my breast firm using it to pull me down harder as he thrusts into me. His hand assaulting my clit as my orgasm builds.

"Come for me, be my good girl and come," he continues his thrusting, moving faster, his hands moving in time with his hips.

I moan loudly as I explode all over him starting to slow down. He gives a couple more pumps putting both hands on my hips as he slams me down as he reaches his limit too, filling me up. I fall against him breathing heavily, looking into his golden brown eyes.

He moves my hair out of my face and cups my cheek pulling my face in for kiss, keeping my body pinned to his. He kisses me soft and sweet, his tongue gliding over mine. He breaks from the kiss, "Gods I missed you." As he smiles, he gently pulls me off him turning the water on so he can use the sponge to clean us both up.

"The feeling is mutual Shadow, it has been awfully boring without my favorite troublemaker." Smiling I stand up drying myself off. He gets out dries off before getting dressed.

Going into the bedroom I chose to wear a black tank top and faded black jeans. The smell of food hits me, "Guess breakfast's ready." I jog into the kitchen, flop down at the table just as Zephyr finishes setting everything out.

Zephyr smiles when he sees me, gives my head a kiss before he sits down across from me. "I hope you enjoy it princess," he points to a glass in front of me, "I warmed up some blood for you as well."

"Thank you, Zephyr," Looking at Lucas I ask, "Do you happen to have any of my back-up supplements?"

He nods, "yeah give me a second," he walks outside to his bike, he comes back a minute later. He sets the pill bottle down before sitting next to me loading up his plate. I grab one of the supplements, taking it and drink some of the blood with it. I load up my plate, eating happily.

After I finish my breakfast I push my empty plate back. "That was really good, Thank you for breakfast Zephyr."

"Always princess, so what do you want to do today?" he asks as he picks up the dishes and take them to the sink.

Lucas perks up, "We can go look for a new place if you want, I know you prefer your own space to retreat to."

I shake my head, "It won't be safe to do that for a while, I need to take some time to talk to the others. It won't be me when we come back here. I think Lilliana needs to talk to you both and come up with a plan for the future." Both of the guys nod. I sit back, closing my eyes disappearing into our mindscape.

Chapter 9
Mindscape

I walk through the doors plopping myself into my seat. I'm spent, I used a lot of energy for the fight, sex with the guys, I'm surprised I was able to eat breakfast!

Lilli comes out of her room and sits down looking at me, "You look wiped...did you overdo it?"

"Haha depends on your definition of overdo it...if it helps, the world isn't in ashes yet." I respond leaning my head back, "I took care of the intruders and then had sex with Zephyr and Shadow."

"Sorry, what?" her jaw drops staring at me, "you.... you fucked Zephyr AND Lucas? Like at the same time or took turns with them separately? Please tell me it's the latter."

I smile internally, "I won't lie to you Lilli, but it's the former."

She shakes her head, Arachne and Ivy come out taking their seats. Ivy sees Lilli looking like she's going to throw up, "What's your deal?"

I laugh looking her way, "I had a 3 some with Zephyr and Shadow after killing some of Dads guards."

Ivy pouts, "that's bullshit, if anyone is supposed to be in a threesome it should've been me!"

◯ "Oh brother," Arachne slaps her forehead with her hand as she shakes her head, "Ivy chill out, I'm sure there's more where that came from."

Lilli stammers before talking clearly, ⚕ "not if I've got anything to say about it. We are not sluts. I would prefer not to be acting like one! If we are done with Lennix, then we wait to find someone better."

I lose it, laughing hard doubling over the table, 🔥 "don't look in the mirror Lilli."

She gets up from her chair and runs out the door leaving it wide open so we can hear what she does as the screen shows on the tabletop. She opens her eyes and runs into the bathroom leaving a stunned Zephyr and Lucas behind. She looks in the mirror before she yelps.

Our body is covered in bites, hickeys, bruises and our wrists have a little imprint from the ropes. Me and the others laugh as she touches each one trying to make them disappear. 🔥 "They aren't going anywhere Lilli," I yell out to her.

She looks in the mirror before giving us a middle finger. We laugh harder, ◯ "go sit your ass down and get back in here." Arachne tells her still laughing.

She sits on the bed and retreats back in here shutting the door, taking her seat. ⚕ "Why.... why did you treat us like this?"

Smiling I shrug, 🔥 "the guys didn't want me to go burn the world down, so they figured I needed to be physically exhausted. It worked. I had the best night ever; however, we need to talk about a dream I had."

I tell them about the dream where I met Selene, they are frozen. I get up heading towards my door,  "I need to recover, I think they want to talk to Lilliana, she's the only one they haven't seen in a while. Shadow misses you and it would make him really happy."

I go through the door shutting it everything going dark around me.

Lilliana's POV

I look at Ivy and Arachne, they both nod to me. "I've enjoyed Zephyr's company too, he's very attentive and kind," Arachne tells me.

Ivy smiles, "he seems to know what we need or want instinctively. He devoured me when I was in charge."

I look at both of them dumbfounded, "who the fuck is this guy?" They shrug going to their rooms shutting the door.

I go through the main door and shut it behind me.

When I open my eyes I'm sitting on the bed, Zephyr and Lucas are on their knees in front of me frowning in concern. Smiling I reach to touch Lucas' cheek. "You came back... I've missed you Lucas..." I throw myself into his arms hugging him tight.

He lets out a breath he was holding, wrapping his arms tight around me, "Lilliana...God's I've missed you. I would always come for you if you called, you know that." He buries his face in my neck, his arms holding me tight against his chest. "We were worried about you for a minute there."

"Sorry," Giggling I look at Zephyr, "Trix told us about your extracurricular activities last night and bragged about all the marks. I prefer to be more reserved and committed."

Lucas laughs releasing me from his bear hug, "That's my girl, so modest!"

Rolling my eyes I stand up looking at both of the guys. "What's the plan for today boys?"

Zephyr looks at Lucas then back at me shrugging, "Whatever the princess wants. What sounds good to you babe?"

I consider my choices for a few minutes, "Well, I think I would like a chance to get to know you more Zephyr and catch up with you Shadow. So how about we go out on an adventure for the day? Just chat, explore the city, maybe even catch up with Sedrick?"

Lucas stands up taking my hand, "Sounds like a wonderful way to spend my day." Zephyr nods as he takes my other hand leaning it up to his mouth giving it a kiss.

Pulling my hands from them, clearing my throat nodding, "Let's get going, I wanna get to the city before lunch rolls around." I look at the clothes Bellatrix put on *it'll do*. After I pull on my sneakers we go out to the cars.

Zephyr walks next to me, "let's take the cougar today." My smile brightens as I get in the passenger seat,

Zephyr gets in the driver's seat, Lucas decided to take his bike.

The drive to the city is silent before Zephyr speaks, "What do you like to do?"

I look out the window, "I like to read, be with friends, and watch the rain. What about you?"

"I like to be outside in nature, work on my car at this shop I own, and spoil a certain princess." He reaches over gently putting his hand on my knee keeping his eyes on the road.

"When we first met, did you try to purposefully ruin my relationship to have me to yourself?" I turn to watch his reaction.

He shakes his head, "no, it was a happy coincidence that your relationship failed but I did not have a hand in it. I'm not a homewrecker. I like you and the others. Did I want you to myself? Of course, you're a wonderful, beautiful person inside and out. Am I willing to share? Yes...within reason. I'm not one for multiple partners, however last night with Trix and Lucas, it didn't bother me as much as I thought it would."

He gives me a genuine smile as we pull into the café parking lot. He parks the car but doesn't get out. He reaches forward gently grabbing my chin, so I'm looking at him. "I fully intend to be by your side till my last breath, if there are others then that's fine. As long as I'm with you I don't care. You are worth it," he gives me a soft kiss.

He pulls away then gets out of the car. Lucas pulls up parking next to us then opens my door for me offering me a hand. "How was the drive Lil?" he asks, wrapping an arm around my shoulder as we walk past the café into the city.

I wrap my arm around his waist smiling, "good, how was the ride?"

"Blissful, one of these days you need to be on the back of my bike." He kisses the top of my head, Zephyr follows next to us holding my other hand. Other people on the sidewalk watch us, staring.

I feel myself shrink into Lucas' arm, he pulls me closer to him, making me feel safer. We walk to a busy diner, Zephyr goes to the counter asking for a booth.

We're standing around waiting for probably 10 minutes before someone walked us to a booth. I sat in the middle as both of the guys sat on opposite sides of me.

A waitress comes up, stands next to Zephyr smiling, putting a hand on his shoulder, not sure why but I don't like her touching him, "Hello welcome to Flo-Anna's, what may I get you started to drink handsome?"

He looks at the menu before looking at me, "I would like a water, my girlfriend would like a coffee with caramel creamer." The waitress looks at me, her eyes narrowing before looking at Lucas trying to bat her lashes at him.

He looks up at her, "I'll have the same as my girlfriend please. I would also like some sugar with mine." Her jaw drops as she takes off in a huff muttering under her breath.

I'm not mad but shocked when they both call me girlfriend as I stare at Zephyr before looking at Lucas, "What did you just call me?"

In unison, like they have rehearsed it, "Our girlfriend." Lucas smiles looking at me, "That's what you are isn't it?" he leans into my ear, "Or do you have mind blowing orgasms with just anyone?"

"Lucas Bane! You watch your mouth," I hide my face in my menu shrinking into the chair. "I'm hungry, wonder what's good?"

Zephyr tilts my menu down so he can see my face, "Burgers and fries are delicious, however I'd rather see you on the menu." He gives me a wink as my face heats, my core starting to throb.

Lucas laughs trying to smother it into a cough as the waitress comes up with our drinks. "What do you want to eat?" She's more hostile now since both guys rejected her.

Zephyr looks at her and hands her all 3 of our menus, "3 of the Flo burgers with fries please."

She writes it down then walks away not saying another word. While I sip on my coffee I look at Lucas, "So how has exile been? How much of the world have you seen?"

"It's been ok, nothing like home. I made it to the beaches of Florida hoping to join a pack, but they made me kick rocks. I decided to just drive around till I found my calling." He looks into his coffee, cupping the mug gently, his leg starts to bounce a little nervously. "I don't want to leave again."

Zephyr leans back into the seat putting an arm up on the back, "Then don't, stay here. There's plenty of space. If you wanna earn your way then you can work with me."

I look at Zephyr trying not to laugh, "He's not a café person and he's a terrible waiter." Lucas glares at me, "no offense but your people skills are lacking."

Lucas lets out a laugh before nodding, "Fair point, she's not wrong. I work better with engines then I do with people."

"I own a garage here in town, I mostly do rebuilds and engine work but I was thinking about branching out and bringing in bikes. Theres surprisingly a lot of demand for bike mechanics." He takes a sip of his water, the waitress sets our food down and my mouth waters at the sight of it.

Lucas stares at his food, "this looks amazing," he starts eating not caring about making a mess on his face.

We each eat our food in silence, Zephyr finishes his food first and wipes his face free of crumbs. Lucas finishes second, I follow shortly after. "That was really good, thank you Zephyr for picking. It was worth it."

"I know," he gives me a cocky grin winking at me, "where do we want to go next?"

Lucas looks at me, "The mall, if I'm going to be sticking around, I'll need more than 2 outfits."

I giggle sitting up straighter, "Oh Shadow, you sure about that?" He sees me smile nodding quickly.

The waitress comes and puts the check down, I go to grab it when Zephyr moves faster, snatching it up. He pulls cash out of his pocket, lays it on the table climbing out of the booth his hand out to me.

Taking his hand, standing next to him, he leans down to give me a soft kiss. "It's not too far to walk but I have a feeling we'll need the car. So, lets head back to the café."

Lucas nods behind me, we head back to our vehicles. As we drive to the mall, I notice it doesn't look very busy, *perfect, I won't get stared at*. I get out of the car, Lucas pulls up beside me. Zephyr waits at the hood of the car for us to join him, together we walk inside to the mall.

We're just starting to walk around when Zephyr nods towards a store, "Let's go to Buckle, that way you can get yourself a couple jeans for work Shadow."

We get inside there's only 3 employees standing around at the counter, Lucas takes off towards the men's section taking care of himself. Zephyr gently folds his fingers with mine pulling me towards the women's section. "He isn't the only one that needs new clothes. You did just leave your whole closet behind."

"No thank you, I need to preserve the money I have left until I get back to work." I give him a smile trying to pull him towards Lucas.

Zephyr laughs before tugging me back to him, "No, you are getting clothes for yourself. Let me spoil you like the princess you are. I know you hate entitlement, but it's not like that. It's me wanting to show you what you are worth."

I look in his eyes seeing he's very genuine about his feelings. Sighing heavily, I nod lowering my head, "where do I even start?"

"Well, 'what does Lilliana like to wear?' would be a good start." He pulls me towards some of the tables with jeans on them.

Looking at the choices, I grab a pair of light blue jeans with a small fade going around the thighs. Moving towards the shirts, I see a cream-colored light sweater and pull my size out taking it to Zephyr. "I prefer clothes that hide my body with neutral colors."

He takes the clothes from me kissing my cheek, "what about Trix?"

Grabbing a pair of black ripped jeans with a blood red tank top putting them in his arms. Seeing what he's trying to get me to do, I get clothes for Ivy, dark blue ripped jean shorts and dark green crop top. For Arachne, I see a beautiful navy-blue sundress, taking them to Zephyr.

He smiles approvingly, nods towards Lucas who has a couple pair of jeans in his hands. Lucas sees the mountain of clothes in Zephyr's arm as laughs, "oh this is going to be more fun than I thought. Those don't look much like your style Z." He puts his jeans on the counter paying for them. He grabs his bag, slings it over his shoulder making his shirt ride up teasing at his muscular chest, I can't help but look.

Zephyr rolls his eyes as he takes the clothes to the register paying for them, he grabs the bags carrying them for me. "Where to next?"

"Hey sweetheart, does your family still host the end of summer masquerade?" Lucas asks as we walk out of the store.

I groan, "Don't remind me, my mother will expect her crown jewel to show up shmooze the crowd with Lennix."

Zephyr grins, "I wonder what would happen if you showed up with someone else this time?"

Lucas laughs, "you just read my mind dude, I would love to announce my return in such a dramatic way."

"No, absolutely not. I won't let you guys get in the middle of my family drama." Shaking my head I go towards the fountain, sitting down looking at the water.

"Princess, they came after you. We want to show them that even though they tried, you're not afraid of them." Zephyr crouches down in front of me, pulls my chin to make me look at him. "They brought us into their drama when they tried to harm you."

Lucas drops his bags next to my feet, crouches down next to Zephyr taking my hands into his, "I also want to show them that even though they tried to keep us apart, they failed miserably so we are stronger than before."

"I'm scared...what if my father tries to hurt one of you? What if he manages to pull me back in and doesn't allow me to leave again?" My hands start to shake in Lucas'. I never realized how much I feared my family before, or how much I care about this stranger and my best friend.

Zephyr leans up kissing me softly, making me hold my breath. After a moment he pulls away stroking my cheek, "We won't let that happen. Nothing will ever keep us from you, we will burn the world to find you if they manage to do so."

He says it with such conviction I trust him. Lucas nods to his words. Nodding I start to calm down, "We are going to need formal wear and masks. I know just the place, luckily it's here in the mall."

Zephyr stands picking up the bags, "let me run these to the car for us and I'll meet you there." He looks at Lucas, "Don't let her out of your sight kid."

Lucas' eyes narrow, he stands up pulling me with him, "I did once, I won't make that mistake again." We head towards the back of the mall, we walk into a beautiful tailor shop. there's dresses on racks, tuxedos along the wall, and spools of fabric on shelves.

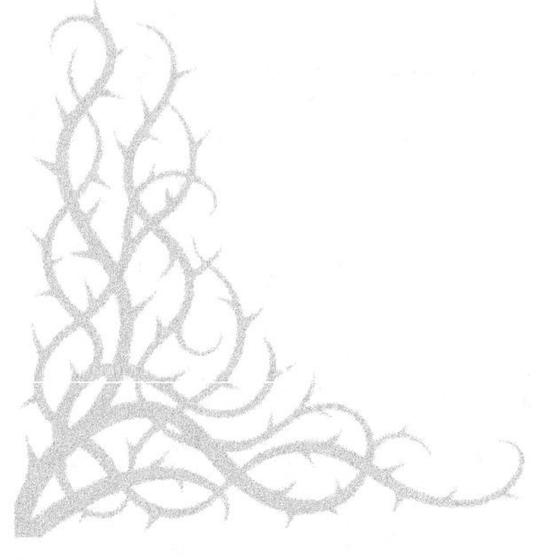

Chapter 10

Lilliana's POV

An old lady greets us without looking up, "Welcome to Fantasy Threads, give me one moment and I'll be right there."

Smiling I head closer to the counter, "Take your time Lisa. I know it's valuable."

At the sound of my voice her head snaps up, a smile lights up her face, "Princess Lilli, is that you?" She tosses the dress she is altering onto the counter, hurries around to me and Lucas. She gives me a polite bow, "I'm happy to see you dear, you make my heart soar seeing you in my store again."

Smiling I give her a hug, "Happy to be here Lisa, I wouldn't go to any other seamstress. I need some help, think you're up for a challenge?"

She raises her eyebrow at me, "Child you know I won't back down from one. What can this old lady do for you?"

"My parent's ball is coming up, I need a dress made and my companions need tuxedos. We also need custom masks." Her eyes light up making me smile more, "you know what I like, and I might need to make a couple...hidden alterations for safety."

"Oh...you make an old lady happy." She looks at Lucas assessing him, "What are you son?"

He clears his throat, "I'm a hybrid, vampire and werewolf. Is this going to be a problem?" He looks at me nervously.

I give him a supporting smile as she walks around him in a circle, "Oh not at all, I just need to know so I can make your outfit suit your needs." She looks at me, "You said companions?" As if he was summoned, Zephyr walks in the door standing next to me, kissing my head. "Oh...you lucky girl." She starts giggling as she walks towards the counter beckoning us to follow.

I get into one of the bar stools, Lucas stands behind me wrapping his arm casually around my waist, Zephyr sits in the stool next to me. "Think you can get it done in 4 days Lisa?"

She waves her hand brushing me off, "Don't insult me Lilliana, you know better. Go make yourself useful and pick the fabric you want for yourself."

Laughing, I push myself up walking towards the wall. My eyes roam over the swathes of color until they catch on a silvery lace that shimmers like diamonds. I grab that before going to find the solid colors. I see a white silk laying the lace over, I don't like how it looks so I find a dark silver satin fabric doing the same thing. It looks better but I'm not in love with it. I walk down the wall before I come across a shimmery black silk fabric that has a glittery shine to it. Smiling I take both bolts of fabric laying them on the counter.

Lisa looks to see what I grabbed smiling, "Child, you're going to have a lot of eyes on you. Now let's make your arm candy look just as good." She looks at Zephyr considering his looks then looks at Lucas. She points to Zephyr and motions for him to follow her as she leads him to the tuxes.

Me and Lucas stay at the counter, a few minutes later she lays down a tux before snapping her finger at Lucas, "Your turn Hun." They walk off, Zephyr laughs giving me a kiss on my cheek.

"She cares about you, told me if she finds out I hurt you she's going to poke me with needles in unfriendly places."

Shaking my head laughing, "She's harmless," I look around waiting, it took longer for her and Lucas to return.

She looks at me smiling. "I'll have your clothes done soon. Just come back for a fitting and we'll make any changes you need."

 Nodding I smile giving her a hug, "Thank you for your help Lisa, I wouldn't dare go to anyone else."

"This is where I'll go for my own formal wear from now on as well. I used to go to the town tailor, but I think I like Lisa more than that crabby old man." Zephyr laughs putting his arm around my shoulder, looking at Lisa, "Thank you for helping us, not to be rude but we are on a date, so I'm going to go back to spoiling this girl."

My face heats as I try to push him away, he doesn't give me much room to budge, then again I'm not really putting much force into it. Lisa's eyes twinkle with joy as she watches us, then looks to Lucas, "What about you dear, what are you off to go do?"

Lucas gives a cocky grin grabbing one of my hands, "He said we are on a date, as in all of us. We are treating this beautiful princess like the queen she actually is, so we best get back to it."

I groan internally trying to hide my face, the guys laugh in unison going back into the mall.

We walk around for a bit going in and out of different stores. I got a new pair of black converse, Lucas and Zephyr got some new boots, and we see that some shops are starting to shut down.

We head to the car when I catch a familiar scent. I start to tremble, Zephyr notices looking down at me, "What's wrong babe?"

I tiptoe to reach his ear and whisper, "I think Lennix is watching us, I don't want to fight him."

His body tenses in anger, but he nods. We walk past the car, heading towards a park with a lake. We all stand looking at the lake and sure enough Lennix walks up behind us about 10 feet away. I turn to see him grinning at us.

"So...the whore found herself some toys huh?" Lennix laughs crossing his arms over his chest. "I knew you were sleeping around if you already got these two."

Zephyr snarls, "Don't talk to her like that. I'll rip your tongue out if you continue to disrespect her."

"Lennix, your all bark no bite. Guess that's to be expected when you're an alpha in all things BUT the bedroom." Lucas snaps back, both of the guys are standing just in front of me where I'm covered but not blocking my view of Lennix.

Lennix's eyes narrow at Lucas, "Shut your mouth mutt. You're not even supposed to be here."

Lucas shrugs, "Maybe not, but if Lilliana needs me, I'll break every law to be there for her."

"Leave Lennix, don't start a fight," I try to plead with him, looking in his eyes. He stares back in hatred.

"I want to kill you, I want to tarnish your body for everyone to see, humiliate you since you humiliated me. However, I'm just here to warn you. I will come for you, and your.... toys won't be able to stop me. Your days are numbered Lilliana." Lennix walks away leaving us behind. I let out a breath I didn't realize I was holding.

Lucas turns to me and touches my cheek, "You ok sweetheart? You want to go home?"

Zephyr is keeping his eyes where Lenix is headed, making sure he doesn't come back this way. I look down at the grass, nodding in response to Lucas. "I'm going to get her back home, see you there." Lucas tells Zephyr while pulling me back in the direction of the vehicles.

Zephyr follows, "I'm going to run to the store and grab something to make for dinner. I'll be behind you guys shortly." He hands me the key to the house as he kisses my forehead, "It'll be ok princess, you're safe with us."

I just nod in response, Lucas grabs a helmet from the bike storage, gently sliding it on my head buckling it for me. He climbs on and gives me a hand so I can climb behind him. He drives carefully back to Zephyr's house.

When we arrive, he helps me off the bike putting the helmet away before leading me inside. Tossing his keys onto the table by the door, he pulls me into a hug. "Are you ok?"

I shake my head wrapping my arms around him tight, I still haven't spoken I can tell he's concerned. He strokes my hair, "Let's sit down on the couch for a little while Lilli." He leads me to the couch, sits down pulling me next to him. I move so I lay my head in his lap curling my feet onto the couch. He grabs the blanket that's on the back of the couch covering me up running his hands through my hair.

Before long I drift to sleep silently, his fingers continuously running through my hair.

I don't know how long I slept for, but I hear Lucas calling my name. When I open my eyes he's smiling down at me, "Hey beautiful. Dinner is ready, do you feel like getting up to eat?"

"Yeah," I sit up stretching, giving a yawn. I can smell whatever Zephyr cooked my stomach growls loudly making Lucas laugh. "I definitely think food is needed," I say while giggling.

We get up and head to the dining room, Zephyr made steak, mashed potatoes, green beans, and has a fresh tossed salad. Sitting down I go to make a plate but Zephyr stops me. "Sit back and relax princess." He makes me a decent size plate before making his own, Lucas has already started to dig in seeming to enjoy it.

I start to eat, enjoying the fact that the steak melts in my mouth. I eat everything on my plate getting more. Zephyr watches me with a smile, Lucas chuckles, and I just devour my next plate without a care.

"Was that good princess?" Zephyr asks while gathering up the dishes off the table.

"Is the grass green?" I chime back while standing up, going to the sink taking the plates from him and washing them off.

Zephyr gives my ass a playful smack which causes me to giggle. I get the dishes washed and drying on the rack. Tossing the towel in Zephyr's face before going back to the living room. Lucas is back in his spot on the couch, so I laid back in his lap. Zephyr sits by my feet pulling my legs into his lap, rubbing my feet.

"So, Lilliana, may I ask the story with your parents?" Zephyr asks while massaging my feet.

Sighing while Lucas runs his hands through my hair trying to ease my anxiety, I respond, "Where should I even start?"

"Whatever is comfortable for you. The beginning would make it easier to follow."

I look up at Lucas smiling as his hands go through my hair, "Well, if we want to start from the beginning then I guess it would be the day I was born. My parents have been the leader of our coven for the last 150 years. They tried to have children countless times. I was the first and only success. I'm 24 years old, my 25th birthday is in a few days. The day I was born was a chaotic one for them. It was a blood moon, they were doing their yearly lockdown, and my mother went into labor. I was born the moment the eclipse reached its peak, it made my parents vulnerable since vampires lose their strength and gifts while wolves get more powerful during the eclipse."

Pausing I take a deep breath fidgeting with my hands, "My mother told me when I got older that the moon goddess Selene had forsaken me. Made me born on the weakest day of our kind, while cursing me with my eyes to show how weak I would always be. My father wanted to keep me hidden, in a cage and under his control. About 8 years ago, after years of trying to broker a treaty for power with the wolves, he was told that the Alpha's son is unmated." Trembling I take a slow breath before continuing, "The alpha told my father that if he has a daughter he can marry off then we can align our families and live a time of peace."

"Lennix was sweet at first, he let me go at my pace, he treated me to flowers, and we went slow. My father and him planned a surprise engagement, had him propose on my 18th birthday. That was the one and only birthday gift I've ever received from anyone so naturally I was over the moon." I close my eyes relaxing at the foot massage, taking a few minutes to just enjoy the feeling.

Lucas strokes my hair, "Take a minute, let me share some of my story while you relax sweetheart." I nod my head in response relaxing even more. "I used to be a part of a small pack, my parents were very kind people, they were the type of leaders every pack or clan should have. Vampires ambushed us when I was 9, my parents died trying to protect me and our pack. A vampire found me hiding in the woods, attacked and fed on me, and gave me some of his blood. He was fully intending on either I turn or I die. I was laying in the mud writhing in pain as the turning process started." He twirls my hair a few times but doesn't stop combing his fingers through my hair, "I was found after I was finished with the transition, brought to Lilli's parents, and joined their coven as a full-fledged vampire. They took me in, and I was their...friend...they were going to allow Lilli to have. She was very sheltered but she is only 2 years older than me, so we got along good. we became very close, I learned I have a shadow transport ability, I would sneak out and take her with me. Her parents saw how much she trusted me, so they trained me to be her personal bodyguard."

"we were inseparable, I took my duty seriously and she hated it. I stopped sneaking us out, I always did what was safest for her. when I turned 13, my life changed in an instant. I didn't feel good, I was temperamental, I was raging on everyone. Her parents sent me away because I assaulted a couple of the guards that were trying to calm me down. I got to the edge of town, the moon reached its peak. I felt a burning pain I had never experienced before, it felt worse than my transition. I thought I lost the ability to shift, so I didn't know or understand what was happening. I ended up having my first shift. Her father followed me, hoping to see I calmed down, he saw what I was and called me an abomination. Told me to never set foot around Lilli again, he never wanted to see my face again, and that because I've served him for years he is giving me the chance to live when I only deserve death." He stops moving his hand, I can feel his body tremble.

Opening my eyes I gently grab his hand bringing it to my mouth, giving it a gentle kiss in his palm. I put it over my heart, breathing slowly, letting it calm him. Sitting up so I can lean against his chest instead of laying in his lap before looking at Zephyr, "we had each other's phone number, so I bugged him until he finally relented and talked to me. He told me what my father did, so I started pushing to get more independence. I never let Shadow go a single day without hearing me. We would talk for hours, and it would almost fill that hole my father created."

Still trembling, Lucas wraps his arms around me giving me a hug across my chest and burying his face in my hair. "I made a deal with Lennix when we got engaged, I wanted to explore and see more of the city. We, my father Lennix and I, came to an agreement, we would have a long engagement so that I could learn about the area. I got a job at a bookstore, fell in love with reading, and did a lot of walking around, just taking in my newfound freedom. Lennix would work all the time and find time for me maybe 3-4 times a week. As time went on it became less and less. My 25th birthday is coming up where I would be recognized as a fully grown vampire. I was groomed to be wed after that happens since that's also when I'll be able to have children."

Zephyr cocks his head a little, "Are you able to have mixed race children? Is that even possible?"

I nod, "Yes and no, often times it's risky because the child could come out too weak for the hybrid blood. But there is also the possibility they could either be a vampire OR a werewolf. Theres not any mixed relationships in this world to really test that theory."

"But your father exiled Shadow for being a hybrid, why would he be willing to allow such a pairing?" Zephyr looks at my feet thinking while still continuing his massage.

"Bellatrix and Arachne think it's a way to create his own army that he can control by being my father and their grandfather. He relishes power and having a family full of hybrids...no one would ever go against him." I close my eyes hearing Trix's voice echo in my mind.

🔥 *He probably was hoping to control us using any children we had as collateral.* She gives a menacing growl.

Taking a deep breath, I open my eyes seeing Zephyr staring at me, "Trix also thinks he planned to control us using our children. He doesn't know about the other girls, I've kept them secret for a very long time. They've helped me when I needed them the most. I've never had a day where I feel lonely because of them. Sure, we don't see eye to eye all the time, but at the end of the day we have each other's back."

Smiling Zephyr nods, "You are a wonderful person Lilliana. The other girls are just as wonderful as you, and I'm happy to have you in my life. I was living a very dull life until you walked in the café, when I fell into your beautiful eyes. You are worth burning this world down for. Whatever you desire, I'll make sure comes to you at all cost."

Lucas lays his chin on my shoulder pulling me closer, "You are my guiding light in my world of shadows. I've always cared about you, I'm happy that you are giving me a second chance to be a part of your life. Any time you find yourself in the dark, I will be the shadows holding you tight, giving you that comfort you desperately need. There isn't a corner in this world where I won't find you."

I close my eyes feeling warmth in my chest I've never felt before. *Is this what love is?* I ask the others.

Arachne answers first, *Yes Lil, this is what love is. We may not ever find our soulmate, but we chose them. They won't let us down.*

I felt whole when the 3 of us were together Lilli, I felt peaceful, happy, and less like I was going to explode on the world, Bella adds in.

Ivy perks up, *they are yummy, that's a plus. But honestly, they seem to know what we need before we do. It's nice to be cared for and accepted.*

I feel like a weight is lifted as they feel the same, sitting up straighter looking at both of the guys. "I don't think I was gifted a mate bond when I was born. It's possible that was one of the downsides of being blessed by the goddess. However, I don't think I care so much. I spent my whole life doing what is proper or what my parent's dictated. I think I want to live my life how I see it...with both of you."

The guys look at each other with a flash of worry before it disappears. They both give me a dazzling smile. At the same time, they both respond, "Sounds perfect."

Chapter 11

I lean forward, gently grab Zephyr by his beard on his chin, pulling him in for a kiss. He meets my gentleness sliding one of his hands onto my neck, his thumb caressing my cheek. Leaning into the kiss more I open my mouth a little, he slides his tongue into my mouth, and I notice he tastes sweet like strawberries.

We make out for a little bit before I get a soft tug on my waist from Lucas. I pull away from Zephyr turning to him, I give Lucas the same soft kiss. He pulls me into his lap, so I'm straddling him when we deepen the kiss. I notice he tastes like mint. I feel him stiffen in his pants as his dick starts to harden.

I pull away from the kiss turning to look at Zephyr who is watching us with a heated gaze. "Let's go to bed. How does that sound?"

Zephyr stands up quickly, picks me up off of Lucas' lap before he carries me like a princess to the room. Lucas right behind him the whole time. When we get to the room I look at Zephyr, "Put me down please," he sets me on my feet. I take one of their hands pulling them closer so I'm standing in the middle of them. "I don't want to rush, I want to enjoy every moment."

They both watch me quietly, I turn to Lucas, my back to Zephyr as I slide his shirt up. He helps me get it over his head, when he brings his hands down he rests them on my cheek. Zephyr puts his hands on my waist, starts to raise my shirt up gliding his fingers over my skin.

After my shirt is tossed to the side I lean forward giving Lucas' neck a kiss, kissing my way down his chest. I unbutton his pants and push them down with his boxers. He kicks his pants to the side.

I stand up turning to face Zephyr. I do the same thing to him and when I stand back up, I grab his face kissing him deeply. He meets my intensity, his hands roaming over my bra. Lucas kisses the back of my neck unsnapping my bra making my breasts exposed to Zephyr's hands. Lucas slides them down my arm and tosses them to the side.

I break from the kiss with Zephyr turning to Lucas, pulling him in for a deep kiss. Zephyr undoes my pants sliding both my pants and underwear down. When he stands back up he glides his fingers slowly up my legs. Sliding his hand to the front of my thigh, he gently cups my mound laying kisses on the back of my neck.

Lucas massages my breast as breaks from the kiss moving to the opposite side of my neck from Zephyr. I lay my head back against Zephyr's shoulder as he slides a finger into my folds finding my clit. He circles it gently, I grab each of their dicks stroking them.

Both of them tense at my touch, I can feel them trying to keep their restraint. Zephyr plays with my clit a little faster so I match his pace by stroking both of them faster. Lucas goes back to kissing me deeply before speaking, "I need to bury myself in you."

Smiling I turn my back to Lucas looking at Zephyr, "Then do it Shadow, may I taste you while he fucks me Z?"

"Baby you don't even have to ask." He grabs my hand pulling me towards the bed as he sits on the end of it spreading his legs.

I bend over, my ass on full display to Lucas behind me and lick the tip of Zephyr's dick. Lucas comes up behind me rubbing my back as he positions himself at my entrance. I slide Zephyr into my mouth, getting a feel for him and start bobbing my head. Lucas grabs my hips sliding inside me slowly, deliberately. Zephyr holds my hair in one hand while rubbing my breast with the other.

Lucas moves his hips pumping in and out of me at the same pace that I'm bobbing on Zephyr's dick. I moan onto Zephyr's dick as my orgasm builds. I can feel his dick twitch as he gets close. I move my head faster, sucking harder. Lucas meets my pace. My walls clamp down on Lucas as I reach my orgasm, I feel Zephyr spill out in the back of my throat, Lucas thrusts one more time deep as he can go before he comes inside me.

I lick Zephyr clean, Lucas pulls himself out giving my ass a gentle tap. I stand and turn to look at him smiling. "Better?"

"Oh sweetheart, that pussy of yours is divine. I'll always be better after being in there. Doesn't mean I'm done though." He gives me a wink, I hear the bed creak.

Zephyr stands up behind me grabbing my waist, "My turn," he pulls me towards the bed and lays me down on the edge at the corner. He lifts my legs so my ankles are by his head and lifts my hips so his dick lines up at my entrance before slowly pushing himself in.

Lucas comes to the edge of the bed next to my head stroking his dick in front of my face, "Want to taste yourself sweetheart? You're still coating my dick nice and wet."

Moaning as Zephyr slides in and out of me slowly but deeper with each movement, I nod my head moving my mouth closer to Lucas with my tongue out. Lucas slides his dick into my mouth and works my mouth the same pace Zephyr is going hitting the back of my throat. Zephyr has a hand on my mound spreading my folds, a finger rubbing my clit fast.

My moans are muffled on Lucas's dick as they both pick up their pace. I feel another orgasm rip through me, they both pump a couple more times before reaching their own. I lick Lucas clean his eyes glint with satisfaction. Zephyr pulls himself out, kisses my ankle, gently putting my legs down.

"Let me grab a rag, then we can go to the hot springs close by." Zephyr goes to get the rag before returning, cleaning me up gently and kissing my thigh when he's done.

He takes my hand, pulling me up slowly. "Lucas I have an extra pair of shorts in the top drawer, why don't you grab that and you can wear it." Zephyr opens one of the bags from the mall, grabs me a 2-piece bikini set he snuck, handing them to me before getting his shorts on.

I slip into my swimsuit, noticing he'd picked out a white set with gold stars. A smile tugs at my lips at the attention to detail. He's wearing red shorts that have a black Japanese dragon on it, Lucas is wearing all-black shorts. Zephyr grabs a couple of towels before he holds a hand out, "We don't need shoes, it's all soft grass. I have a pathway we can follow."

We follow him out walking through the woods a couple yards and we come to a beautiful spring that has a waterfall leading to the river. The sun has started to set so it's bathing the mountainside in a beautiful shade of yellow and orange.

I walk towards the spring and dip a toe in, feeling the warmth. "This feels phenomenal." I walk into the spring finding a bed of flat rocks I can sit on before settling myself there. Lucas looks at Zephyr with a grin, asks him a silent question to which Zephyr nods.

Zephyr walks in swimming to me, crouched down so his shoulders are under the water. He looks up at me as he grins. I hear a holler before a huge splash as Lucas runs jumping into the spring like a cannonball.

I wipe the water off my face laughing as Lucas comes up, he laughs watching me. "That was worth it. This really does feel good." He floats around and I lay my head back on the rocks looking at the sky watching the colors as the sun continues to set.

Zephyr disappears under the water, and I hear a yelp. I sit up to look seeing that Zephyr flipped Lucas into the water, they are wrestling, having fun.

The sun fully sets so we head back to the house. Instead of going back in, Zephyr takes his towel and lays it out in the grass laying on it, looking at the stars. I watch him then look at Lucas. Lucas goes inside blowing me a kiss.

I blow him a kiss back, laying my towel down next to Zephyr. I lay on the towel watching the stars with him.

We sit there in silence, his hand searches for mine in between us, when he finds it he intertwines our fingers together. We lay there for a while before he speaks, "I wonder who attacked you the other night, I was hoping when you told me more about your past it would make sense. But I'm just left with more questions."

"I don't know, from what Bella could share I know for sure they are evil, felt malicious towards me, and a magic user. Other than that, I'm not sure, I don't know a lot of witches or wizards. They generally steer clear of my kind." I watch as the moon makes its appearance, still have 4 days till the full moon...which is also my birthday. I take a slow breath closing my eyes.

I'm wiped out, I feel myself drifting off when Zephyr rolls over, crawls on top of me looking down into my eyes holding himself up on his arms. "You look absolutely radiant my love." He leans down giving me a soft and sensual kiss.

I wrap my arms around his neck kissing him back closing my eyes. His knee slides in between my legs so I open them up a little more. He deepens the kiss pressing his hips to mine, I can feel his dick harden. I curl my fingers in his hair spreading my legs more inviting him in. He uses one hand to move his shorts down enough for his erection to spring free, he slides my bikini to the side.

He positions himself to my entrance not taking his lips off mine and pushes himself in with one smooth stroke. My grip in his hair tightens as I moan into his mouth. I like it when the guys share me, but I treasure these moments alone just as much. He makes love to me under the stars drawing it out as long as we both can last. We both reach our orgasms together after 20 minutes.

I'm left breathless when he finally breaks the kiss, my grip on his hair loosens and he looks into my eyes. I see him wanting to say something but stopping himself. "What is it Zeph?"

"I don't want to scare you away by moving too fast." He strokes my cheek smiling.

I lean up to kiss him softly, "You won't, I'm not going anywhere Zeph, you're stuck with me and my crazy counterparts."

He laughs and smiles, "I love you Lilliana Nightshade. And all your counterparts."

I look into his eyes looking for deception but find none, *He says he loves us...isn't that too soon?* I ask the others.

No. I heard them all say collectively. I smile before give him another kiss, "I love you to Zephyr Volos. So do all my counterparts."

He lets out a breath of relief and stands up pulling me with him, "Let's get to bed, it's getting pretty late."

I nod yawning in response. We walk in and head to the bedroom. Lucas is asleep on the bed, looks like he is sleeping soundly. I crawl into the bed quietly snuggling into his side wrapping my arm around his waist. As if on instinct his arm wraps around me pulling me close but not waking up.

Zephyr crawls in bed behind me and lays down putting his hand on my waist kissing the back of my head.

I drift to sleep easily feeling more at home and safe than I ever have before.

Dream State

I open my eyes while lying in bed. I see the sun rising as the colors dance around the room. Sitting up I look around, I'm not in Zephyr's room. I seem to be in a beautiful cabin that looks similar to my mindscape cabin. Music is playing softly in another area, getting up I follow the music.

I see a woman sitting at a piano playing a serene tune. I sit down next to her watching her hands, lost in the melody.

"Hello Lilliana. How are you child?" the woman says.

She finishes the song before she looks at me smiling, she's beautiful and flawless. "Confused, but happy...I think. Selene I presume?" I ask.

She nods, "I'm very proud of you for finally sticking up for yourselves and carving your own path. You are growing to be a wonderful queen I know you to be."

"I'm no queen, nor do I aspire to be one. I just want to live my life." I look down letting out a shaky breath.

"Maybe so, but the time will come when a ruler needs to step up and unite the world from chaos. One who will rule with their heart and head, not greed and ambition." She starts to play another slow song, "True leadership comes from knowledge, personal trials, experience, and passion to encourage the best in others, don't believe me? Ask Lucas, he knows what true leadership is. You may not be ready now. But one day, you will be, and it will be a day this world will never forget."

I cover my face in my hands shaking, "Why me? I'm not strong enough and because I don't have a true mate bond I'll never be strong enough."

"It should be you because even though the world has thrown trials at you time and time again...you still stop to enjoy the little things in life. You see the good in people even when everyone else sees the bad. You give people hope and light when the world itself is dark and hopeless." She continues playing, "You are stronger than you think. Trust in yourself, trust in the other girls. I put you guys together to build each other up and strengthen your resolve. Unlock your powers, unlock your potential, and nothing will ever stand in your way."

The song tapers off to a slow end, when I move my hands from my face Selene is gone. I look around and see a beautiful snowy owl on the windowsill. I walk to it and it flies off. I try to follow it, running.

It flies off higher, I feel a tug in my chest telling me to keep going. I close my eyes take a couple deep breaths and run as fast as I can. I see a cliff and the owl keeps flying.

I skid to a stop at the edge of the cliff. The owl turns to watch me before flying off towards the moon. The tug in my chest gets tighter so I jump without thinking.

I feel the wind rushing past me as I fall down the cliff, I close my eyes tight as I see the rocks at the bottom wishing I could fly. I feel a rush of wind thinking I'm about to hit the rocks but it doesn't come.

When I open my eyes I'm floating above the rocks just a few feet away. Laughing I look up into the sky and see the owl overhead. It takes off flying, I take a breath before flying after it.

After a while I start to feel tired and weak. I freefall over the ocean, when I hit the water I'm snapped awake back in bed with Zephyr and Lucas.

Lilliana's POV

I jolt out of bed sitting up straight waking Zephyr and Lucas up with a start. "What is it?! What's wrong?!" They both start asking quickly.

I take a shaky breath, "Sorry, I dreamt I was falling and hit the middle of the ocean. It felt so real that I feel like I just belly flopped into the water."

Lucas wraps his arms around me, kisses my cheek, "It's ok baby, you're here, your safe with us. Breathe."

I slowly calm down in his arms my breathing evening out. "I'm getting a little hungry, is there any blood left?"

Zephyr goes to the kitchen and comes back shaking his head. "No babe there isn't. Before I go to get you some can you tell me why you can't feed on people?"

Chapter 12

Lilliana's POV

I move out of Lucas's arms, sit against the headboard pulling my knees to my chest resting my chin on them.

I watch them both for a moment taking a deep breath before nodding. "Promise not to look at me different?"

Zephyr laughs a little putting a hand on my leg, "Baby girl... you have 4 personalities, each one a bad ass in their own right, have beautiful eyes of different colors, and were blessed by the moon goddess. There is nothing in this world that would make me look at you differently." Lucas nods in agreement and puts his hand on my other leg.

With both of them giving me comfort and support I feel ready to open up more. "My parents told me that part of my curse is I'll kill anyone I bite. Even my fated mate during the mating process. I was always terrified to try it but a rogue vampire attacked me when I was 8. I don't remember much of it except that I lost a significant amount of blood, so I ended up in a starving state. I lost myself to a blood rage and attacked one of my father's guard when he found me, I fed on him." I bury myself in my knees trembling, "I passed out after I reached my fill, when I came to, my father told me I murdered the guard. He berated me, telling me I should not have run off from my guards and made myself vulnerable to attack but because I did his death was my fault." I feel tears streaming down my face.

The bed shifts as both of the guys sit next to me wrapping their arms around me in a cocoon. I sit there crying for a few more minutes shaking. ⬦ *It wasn't your fault Lilli, we weren't there to protect you yet. But ever since then we came together and now we will make sure it won't ever happen again.* Arachne speaks to me, trying to calm me down.

I sit up a little bit wiping my face while looking at Zephyr. "Ever since then I've been terrified to try again. I'm scared I'll become a monster."

"Lil... you are not a monster, nor will you ever be one." He wipes my tears away gently tilting my chin so I can see into his eyes better, "I also think that your father lied to you. I'm willing to try to prove otherwise."

Lucas gently lets me go and moves to the side. Zephyr pulls me into his lap, so I'm straddling him. "I'm not scared of you Lil, I trust you, all you need to do is trust me and yourself. You need to feed, you won't be as strong as you should be without fresh blood."

I search his eyes for hesitation but frown when I don't see any. Taking a shaky breath, I lean down towards his neck baring my fangs. ⬦ *Lilli are you sure?* Ivy warns me. I get ready to bite when I feel pain in my stomach. I pull away and it goes away just as fast.

"I'm sorry, I can't." I scramble to get off his lap and run into the bathroom slamming the door shut locking it.

I hear Zephyr mutter something, him and Lucas have a hushed conversation. Sliding onto the floor of the bathroom I wrap my arms around my legs crying silently.

Lucas's POV

I watch as Lilli runs and locks herself in the bathroom. Zephyr's shoulders slump in defeat, "I was really hoping she would try." Zephyr says looking at me, "She needs fresh blood. She would be unstoppable."

I nod looking at the bathroom door, I can hear her tears dropping onto the floor. Taking a slow breath, "I'm going to go look into it. I know just the place to look. Try to see if she will drink your blood if you put it in a cup instead of actually biting you. May not be the same but we can't force her to mark us Zephyr. Not even without telling her the truth."

He nods and leaves the room. I find the bags we got from the mall, grab a black pair of jeans, black shirt, and my combat boots. I get dressed and walk to the door crouching down, "Lilli, Zephyr is going to get you a glass of blood. Try to see if that helps. I'm going to run an errand. I'll be back soon sweetheart."

I hear a sniffle in response but nothing else. I see Zephyr return with a glass and some blood, "I'll be back soon, keep an eye on her for me. If you need me just call." I disappear sinking into the shadows.

I travel through the shadows listening, I finally hear the voice's I'm looking for. I blend into the shadows of Julian's office and hear him talking to Amelia.

"Where is the witch, she needs to make sure the curse is strong enough before the runt's birthday," Julian asks Amelia. He is sitting at his desk with papers all over it.

"She is proving hard to find. If Lennix would've kept her under control then this wouldn't be a problem. Why did you match her with someone so incompetent?" Amelia is looking out at the city dressed as if she is ready to step in front of a crowd of people as a queen.

Julian grumbles rubbing his temples, "Because our first choice is no longer suitable. I am surprised he survived the transition. Lennix screwed up by neglecting her for too long, so she took notice. I need her to marry him, then have a couple of his mutts. Once she does that we can kill him and rule over this world. If the curse continues to wane then we can use the spawn to control her."

Amelia turns, walks to Julian and spinning his chair enough for her to sit into his lap. "This insolent daughter of ours is getting on my nerves. Can we call Lennix and get the plan fixed?" Just then the phone rings loudly.

Julian answers, a mischievous grin appears on his face, "Wonderful, thank you Chelsea. I'll be waiting for your arrival."

My ears perk up, I don't like that smile on his face. Amelia smiles, "She finally returned our call? When should I expect her my love?"

He runs a hand down her back causing her body to shiver, "She will be here in an hour, with a gift in tow." He grabs a fist full of her hair making her neck arch and kisses her throat. "Plenty of time to fill you up."

She smiles, "Ravage me my King."

Without another word he spins her around, bends her over his desk scrambling all of the papers off it. He slides her dress up, unbuttons his pants, pulls his dick free and slams into her with such force the desk shifted. I close my eyes hearing skin on skin, moaning, screaming, yelps of pain before a deafening roar as I assume Julian climaxes.

I wait for a few moments of silence before opening my eyes and see them both dressed and decent. They go back to what they were doing before there is a loud crash into the door as Lennix bursts through.

I feel rage bubble inside me watching him strut like he owns the world. I keep my breathing even and quiet watching as he sits in one of the chairs in front of Julians desk.

"Your bitch of a daughter got the message. I hope she gets her ass back here soon." Lennix informs the Nightshades. Julian raises an eyebrow before nodding in agreement.

He goes through a couple more pages of paperwork on his desk, Amelia sits on the lounge chair behind him watching Lennix. "Why did you loosen your hold on her heart? We told you that she is a very vulnerable person. The best way to control her is through her emotions." Julian informs Lennix, who does not take kindly to being told what to do and it shows when he sits up straighter and his muscles tense in his jaw.

"I've got too much to deal with that doesn't include your emotional train wreck that's your daughter. You told me to make her fall in love, so I did. I spoiled her any time we were together. She got too into her head and suddenly got confidence to stand up to me."

Julian looks up from his papers a look of confusion on his face, "She has no confidence. How could she gain any strength or have a will to fight? We kept her weak by limiting her blood source! You had better fix this Lennix Wolfe or so help me I'll make you regret the day you were born just like your cousin."

Amelia walks up behind Julian wrapping her arm around his shoulder, "Calm down my love, maybe Chelsea can fix it, and we will have her back under our control. As long as she doesn't feed the curse will stay strong."

I get ready to leave when I hear the door knock, a beautiful young girl in a bright purple robe walks in. She sits down crossing her legs. "I hope I'm not interrupting."

"Not at all Chelsea, we are happy you are here. We were just discussing you." Amelia says as she stands next to Julian's side. "Apparently the curse isn't as prominent it used to be. She is getting stronger."

Chelsea raises her eyebrow, "I know. When I met her she had a stronger aura than before. I tried to shoot her with a poisoned dart, but she managed to dodge it. I ran off to gather more information."

Lennix perks up, "You were the one who attacked her 5 days ago?"

She looks at him curiously, tilting her head, "You know about that?"

He nods, "Yeah she messaged me frantic because she was attacked and blacked out. I assumed it was a nightmare since she has those frequently. You had her pretty scrambled."

"Not scrambled enough. I was interrupted and barely got away. She is getting too strong. I'm not sure if I can strengthen her curse without being close. I've got a way in too.... using her own weakness against her," she snaps her fingers, a man is on his knees in front of the desk with a hood covering his face. She pulls the hood off and my heart aches for Lilliana. Lennix's jaw drops before he starts laughing like a maniac.

Sedrick looks up blinking his eyes a couple times confused then sees Chelsea and smiles like he is in a trance.

Chelsea rolls her eyes and pushes him to the side, so he topples over, "This is Sedrick Moranth, leader of the Bear clan here. He also happens to be a good friend to Lilliana. If he calls her, she will show up. I can use him to get her in range."

"Wow, you are one cold hearted bitch. I love it, so you're also the girlfriend we were supposed to have a double date with." Lennix sits back smiling amused.

"I was using him as an opportunity to check on her status, noticed she felt her stronger than usual. I tried to play the jealous girlfriend, but she didn't seem to be fazed by it. When I fix the curse, Lennix, you will need to be there. If you help her relax and heal mentally from the damage, she will forgive you and will never leave you again. Keep her close by this time. I don't know what allowed the curse to weaken but I'm trying to find out." She crosses her arms and the look in her eyes is one that sends shivers down my spine.

Lennix thinks, "Does it have anything to do with the 2 guys she won't leave behind?"

Chelsea's neck snapped so fast you would think it would fly off when she turned to look at him, "what guys?"

"Her ex-friend, bodyguard, would-be alpha Lucas Bane. He came back to town." Julian responds telling her about me.

"The other guy is a nobody, he works at a café and as a waiter for Francesco's," Lennix also tells her...*Zephyr*.

Her face goes pale, "One of them has to be her fated mate. That can be the only way the curse loses its effectiveness aside from removing it myself. Which one is the mate?" She asks both of the men. They shake their head shrugging in response.

"As long as she doesn't mark either of them, the bond is only one way. The curse blocks her strength and the mate bond. If I can hurry and reinforce the magic then Lennix can keep her away from both of the guys until we learn which one is the mate and kill them. As long as they are alive, they will be able to break the curse." She sits back contemplating, I've heard enough.

I need to get back to the others quickly, I go deep into the shadows towards the bright light in the center. Knowing it's Lilliana I move faster towards it.

I come out of the shadows, she is laying on the bathroom floor curled into a ball. I gently scoop her up carefully, trying not to wake her, open the bathroom door laying her on the bed and tucking her in.

Zephyr comes into the room; he looks ragged and worn out. I put a finger to my lips telling him to be quiet and point at the deck.

We go outside sitting down in the chairs, I pull out a cigarette and light it up taking a couple drags before he breaks the silence, "She took the blood but refused to come out. She cried herself to sleep. I don't know what to do or how to help."

I pinch the bridge of my nose taking a deep breath, "It's going to get worse, however you were right. Her parents did lie to her, they stopped her from being able to feed because she got too strong for them to control."

"What do you mean?" he asks looking at the bright forest, it's close to dinner time, so the sun is still visible over the mountains and forest.

I tell him what I heard and what is being planned. I can feel heat coming from Zephyr as he gets angrier and angrier with each word. I turn looking in the window watching Lilli sleep. "You were the catalyst they were not prepared for." I look at Zephyr taking a long drag of my cigarette finishing it before tossing the butt into the gravel pathway. "Then I increased it when she called me back. We make her stronger, braver, more capable. Her birthday is in 4 days...we can keep her here until that happens. The witch said she has to strengthen the curse before her birthday. If she makes it till then without seeing her...the curse breaks and she will be free forever."

"She won't stand for that Lucas. You know that. We need to give her the best life possible, that means not hiding. You also said she can mark her mate to break the curse...so if she marks us...and we mark her..." He trails off lost in thought.

I let out a sigh leaning back against the chair, "she needs to be willing and open. We need to reinforce her trust in us...I think I have an idea, but we can't tell her about this, she will push us away to protect us."

Zephyr nods, "I'll follow your lead kid."

"We need to go check on our clothes at the mall, can you get us a table at Francesco's?" I ask standing up brushing the ash off my pants.

"Consider it done, get dressed in some nice clothes. No bike this time, I want us all together." He stands up, grabs his phone from his pocket making a call. I go inside, grab a nice black button up shirt to wear with my jeans I've got on slipping it on. I leave it unbuttoned as I go to Lilli stroking her cheek softly, "Lilli, sweetheart it's time to wake up."

Lilliana's POV

I hear my name and slowly open my eyes. Someone carried me to bed, I sit up, seeing Lucas dressed nicely. I smile, "You clean up good handsome."

He gives me a kiss brushing his finger on my cheek. "Thank you baby girl. Time for you to get dressed. We are going to go check on our clothes for the ball and go out to dinner."

"Dinner? Is it that time already?" I look around and spot the clock on the wall. I slept half the day and frown. "I'm sorry I didn't spend enough time with you guys. I shouldn't have slept all day." Lucas cuts me off with a kiss making me freeze in place.

"Don't apologize Lil, you are fine. No one is upset or hurt. Now get that sexy ass up and dressed." He pulls me out of the bed and smacks my ass grinning.

I roll my eyes, grab a cream-colored sundress out of the bags. Lucas leaves the room, and I get dressed. I put on some heels that match the color and brush my hair before going to the living room.

Lucas buttoned up his shirt, talking with Zephyr who is wearing black pants and a dark burgundy button up shirt that's buttoned as well. They turn to look at me and both give me their widest grins.

"You look amazing Lilliana." Zephyr says walking to me and taking one of my hands laying a kiss on my knuckles.

Lucas opens the door holding an arm out for us to lead the way, "Drop dead gorgeous Sweetheart."

I feel my cheeks heat as we load into the car. We drive to the mall in silence enjoying the ride. When we park Lucas opens my door for me offering me a hand. I take it stepping out, looping my arm in his. We walk into the mall and head towards Lisa's shop.

When we enter Lisa look's up and smiles seeing that it's us. "Aww you guys look absolutely stunning. I hope you're ready to see your clothes!"

Zephyr nods, "I think we should keep each other in suspense. So would it be ok if we each tried them on in secret?"

"I agree," Lucas perks up looking down at me grinning. "I would rather have a big reveal to stop my heart."

Lisa grabs my hand as she drags me to the changing rooms shutting the curtains. She opens the closet door and pulls out the dress she made for me...my jaw drops.

She looks at me concerned and frowns, "Do you not like it?"

"Are you kidding, it's gorgeous. I love it! I think the boys are going to have trouble keeping me out of the spotlight." I gently take it from her trying it on. It fits perfectly and flows just like I wanted it to. I lift up one of the legs and grin seeing the hidden sheaths for Bellatrix's daggers. "I appreciate you making the alterations for me, I know it was a rather odd ask."

She smiles as she stands behind me checking her work, "I think this might be my greatest creation yet. You are a divine princess."

I turn to see her bowing down, shaking my head I pull her up smiling. "Don't do that please," I ask her nicely. I carefully pull the dress off handing it to her, she puts it in a blacked out garment bag. I get dressed before carrying the bag to the counter setting it down gingerly.

Zephyr goes to try his and comes back with his bag laying it on top of mine. Lucas does the same. When all the clothes are laid on the counter Lisa looks at me smiling. "I'll be at the ball, can't wait to see all of you together. I think you will cause a bit of a ruckus."

Zephyr hands her his credit card to pay for the clothes, she gives him the receipt, and we carry our clothes to the car. Zephyr pops the trunk and we each lay them out gingerly.

Chapter 13

〜 *Lilliana's POV*

We get back into the car driving to Francesco's, Zephyr opens my door for me this time. We walk in together, Zephyr looks at the hostess, "Volos party of 3 please."

The hostess nods then grabs 3 menus, "Right this way please." She leads us to a booth setting the menus down for us. Zephyr lets me slide inside the booth and sits next to me. Lucas sits across from us watching us with a smile.

I'm shocked that the two of them don't show signs of jealousy. I haven't heard of men being so willing to share a woman before. I open the menu as a waiter comes to our table. Zephyr puts his hand on my shoulder, "What would you like to drink love?"

I look up from the menu, "Water please." Zephyr smiles as he shakes his head ordering himself an old fashioned. Lucas orders a bottle of beer looking at his menu.

When the waiter brings the drinks we each place our order. I order the shrimp and chicken alfredo, Lucas orders a steak with the house made mushroom sauce and baked potato, and Zephyr orders the surf and turf dish with steak and lobster.

He takes our menus before he goes to put our order in. Zephyr strokes my thigh taking a sip of his drink. "How are you feeling princess?"

I take a sip of my water smiling, "Better thank you. I was actually curious, why don't the two of you get jealous of each other?"

Zephyr laughs and looks to Lucas before looking back at me, "Because sharing you makes you happy. If it makes you happy then what is there to be jealous of?"

"Exactly. We only care about being whatever you need us to be, and we each offer you something special. Individually we have a connection but together we are stronger." Lucas smiles before taking a drink of his beer.

"So, you both want to share me until we get tired of each other?" I look down at my hands in my lap, *my fear is they will grow bored and find someone else*. That's what Lennix ultimately did.

"Absolutely not. We want to share you until our final breath in this life. And then share you again in the next." Zephyr sits closer to me, turns my face to his giving me a passionate kiss.

The waiter drops our food off, silently walking away from the display of affection. Lucas slides his legs under the table where our feet meet brushing his ankle with mine.

We break from the kiss, Zephyr's eyes are darker tinted with lust. He clears his throat and pushes himself back in front of his food.

We start to eat our food. We eat in silence enjoying our dishes. When we finish Zephyr settles the bill and stands up offering me his hand. I get up and loop my arm around Lucas's arm.

We leave the restaurant going back to the car. We start the drive home in silence again, I lay my head back against the seat watching the night sky as we drive by.

When we arrive back at the house Lucas opens the door for me and offers me a hand while Zephyr gets the clothes from the trunk. Lucas looks at me smiling, "What would you say about going for a walk with me Lil?"

I nod slipping off my heels handing them to Zephyr who takes them without a word and goes inside. "Lead the way Lucas."

He folds his fingers in mine, and we walk towards the river. We spot a dry patch of grass, Lucas sits down with one of his knees propped up and his legs spread apart. He tugs my hand pulling me in between his legs holding my back to his chest as we look out at the beautiful river.

"I've always dreamt seeing something like this with you...watching the moon glisten on your fair skin, your smile lighting up my world, holding you in my arms before I confessed to you how much I love you." He rubs my arms slowly, my breath catches when he says the end. "Reality is even better, because being able to physically hold you is better than any dream I could conjure up."

He tilts my face so I can look into his eyes, he strokes my jaw softly, "I love you Lilliana, I always have. You are my home, my light, and my reason to be a better person."

Tears well in my eyes, I turn my body so I am partially sitting on his lap now. "I love you too Lucas, I know it has been such a long time but a part of me went missing when you left. I feel like you brought me back to life."

His eyes light up in joy, he leans down giving me a deep passionate kiss. His tongue demanding entrance into my mouth, I part my lips allowing it to enter. He kisses me deeper pulling me fully into his lap, so I'm straddling him.

I feel his dick harden underneath me and break from the kiss breathing heavy. He uses the chance to kiss my throat his hands sliding my dress up to my hips.

I reach down unbuttoning his pants sliding them down as best I can his dick springing free. He sucks on my neck and uses both hands rip my underwear, tossing it on the grass. I lay my hands on his shoulder and slowly sit on his dick sliding it as deep into my pussy as I can.

He grabs my hips to lift me up slowly before slamming me back down hard. My hands go into his hair holding on tight, I lean my mouth down to his kissing him deeply. I grind against him as he pulls me up each time, letting him control the pace I ride his dick. He groans into my mouth as I moan into his.

His grip tightens on my hip so I start moving my body faster without his help. He slams me down harder as each moment passes, he bites my lower lip kissing down to my neck leaving me kisses and bites all over. My climax reaches its peak, I come undone all over him. He pulls me down hard as he reaches his orgasm coming deep inside me.

I breathe heavy laying my forehead on his, not wanting to move just yet. He strokes my hips gently, gives me a soft kiss and smiles. "I really do love you Lilli."

"I love you too Lucas, let's get inside, I'm getting pretty tired." I give a soft laugh, gently pulling myself off his lap.

He groans as he pulls his pants back up standing up. "Fine but I feel like a shower might be in order."

"Alright deal, but no more fooling around, I'm really tired." Laughing I walk back to the house going towards the bathroom.

Zephyr is laying on the bed scrolling through his phone and looks up when he hears me come in. He gives me his usual charming smile, "Hey there beautiful, how was your walk?"

I blush shaking my head going in the bathroom turning on the shower. He laughs behind me as Lucas comes back inside as well. "It was interesting. Nightfall wasn't the only thing to come tonight."

I groan hearing what Lucas said, undressing before getting into the warm shower closing my eyes relishing in the steady stream. I hear the shower door open as both of the guys step in next to me. "Behave both of you." I tell them both barely suppressing a giggle.

They both grin holding their hands up in fake surrender. "Yes princess," Zephyr responds. I wash my hair and body, the guys take care of themselves. Any time someone needed under the showerhead to rinse off they would casually brush against my breast or ass, I'm sure it was more intentional than not, but they get props for not misbehaving.

when we are all done Zephyr steps out first drying off before wrapping a towel around his waist. He tosses Lucas a towel and holds one out for me.

I step out wrapping the towel around me, going into Zephyr's closet my mouth dropping as I see all of our new clothes added to it. I find one of Lucas's T-shirts, put it on and find my underwear sliding it on.

I exit the closet, the guys are on the bed waiting, only in boxers. "Did you make room for us in your closet?"

Zephyr smiles nodding, "This is your home now. Until we get a contractor and do a remodel we will unfortunately be sharing a closet, but I made sure it happened for you."

I jump on top of him and give him a big kiss, "Thank you Zeph. It means a lot." He gives me a tight hug. He pushes me off to his side a little, so I lay on the bed, he lays my head on his chest kissing the top of it.

Lucas curls up behind me wrapping an arm around my waist kissing my shoulder. "Good night sweetheart. I love you dearly."

"I love both of you," I reply back with a yawn snuggling into Zephyr's side.

I wake from a dreamless sleep, see Zephyr still asleep, his hold on me relaxed. I carefully slide out of his arm and turn toward Lucas. He's got a smile on his face, but I can tell he's still asleep due to his snoring. I stifle a giggle and crawl out of the bed not to disturb either of them.

I head to the kitchen and see the sun start coming up. My fangs are aching from hunger. I look for the bottle of supplements taking one with a glass of water. I look in the fridge thinking about what to cook for breakfast but nothing sounds good, so I shut the fridge and sit on the couch.

I retreat into my mindscape hoping to let someone else take control. I never do well with hunger, I need someone else to keep us from making mistakes.

⚊ MINDSCAPE

I walk through the door and sit at the round table scratching at the wood with my nail. The others file out of their rooms and sit down quietly...they feel it too. ⚊ "I don't know how I can keep going like this."

Bellatrix leans forward folding her hands in front of her. 🔥 "We need to feed, that's all there is to it. Let me take over. I don't feel guilt for killing someone. I'll feed on someone worth killing, that won't be missed."

💧 "That isn't acceptable Trix. Don't suggest that to her again," Arachne chastises her. "We are not murderers; we won't become one."

Ivy rolls her eyes, 🍃 "Just feed on one of the guys, they are strong it won't kill them to lose a little bit of blood. Zephyr already fed us some of his yesterday so just bite from the source."

I cover my face with my hands taking a shaky breath, ⚊ "I don't want to hurt them... I don't want to risk losing them."

Ivy gives a huff standing up, heading towards the main door, 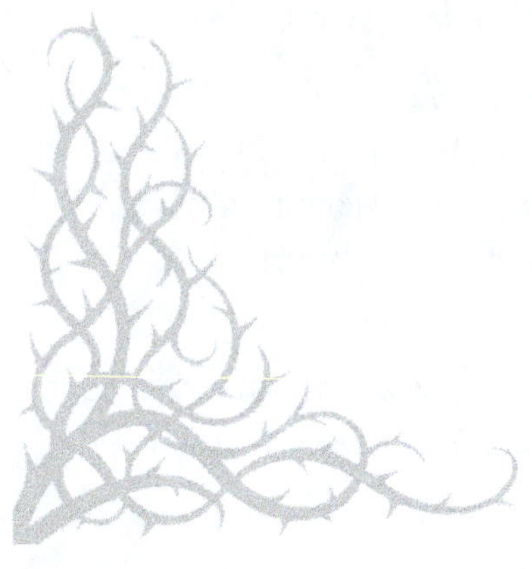 "Such a chicken, wise up for once Lil. We won't hurt them or lose them. They were begging for us to feed on them yesterday, so for once shut up and stop overthinking."

"Ivy.... What do you think you're doing?" Arachne asks with a warning tone.

She shrugs going through the door shutting it before any of us could react. She didn't block us out so we can watch and listen if we choose to.

Chapter 14

Ivy's POV

I open my eyes and head to the bedroom where the guys are still sleeping. *Hmm...if I'm going to eat I think I want to work up an appetite first. Wonder if a good old-fashioned game of hide and seek will work.* I pull on some sneakers and quietly write a short note stating "first one to find me gets a prize" leaving it on the pillow where Lilli slept.

I go out the porch door, look around seeing the mountains and the forest. Deciding to jog I head to the forest, looking around for a good place to lay low. I see where the forest meets the river, a waterfall can be heard. *If I remember right...there is a cave inside...*I head to the waterfall, when I get to the cliff I jump landing at the bottom with a soft thud.

I climb the rocks to get into the cave, smiling when I see a clean spring inside. I take off my clothes tossing it onto a pile of moss and rocks to keep them dry before getting into the water floating with my eyes closed.

Zephyr's POV

Something tugs at me so I open my eyes. Looking around I notice Lilli isn't in bed anymore but there is a note. Grabbing a pillow, I use it to hit Lucas in the face startling him awake.

I give him the note, getting up to walk around the house sniffing to see if I can smell her. The scent is light, but she isn't here, I can tell. "She's a naughty little minx this morning isn't she?"

Lucas comes up behind me laughing, "This sounds like Ivy, she loves games. Thrill of the chase she calls it."

"Chase.... ahhhh that's right. First time we had sex I had to chase her through the house to claim my prize...my oh my she's feisty. Well let's not leave her disappointed." I grab some sneakers and go to the back door sniffing the air.

Lucas comes behind me grabbing my shoulder, he sinks us into the shadows. When he pulls us out of the shadows he puts his finger over his lips telling me to be quiet pointing in front of us.

Ivy is floating in a shallow spring, body on full display. She hasn't given any indication she's sensed us yet. I quietly slip my clothes off and edge closer to the water carefully. Lucas does the same thing going the opposite direction.

Ivy's POV

I wonder how long till the guys find me, sure hope they don't sleep all day. I'll turn into a raisin if I stay here.

No sooner as I finish that thought, than a splash is heard as hands pull me into their arms. I flail my arms, trying to wipe the water off my face so I can open my eyes when another pair of hands grabs my hands pulling them tight behind my back.

The first pair of hands wraps some sort of fabric around my face blocking my eyesight, another piece of fabric is wrapped around my face going into my mouth muffling my yell that was about to escape.

I get a hard smack on my ass, my wrists are tied behind my back. A husky voice whispers into my ear, "Found you, naughty minx."

My body relaxes instantly hearing Zephyr's voice. I grin inwardly, *they are good.* I lean towards Zephyr, when I move I get a rough yank by the bindings on my wrist making me falter backwards against Lucas.

"We did not tell you that you can move." He gives a hard smack to my ass, it echoes in the cave, I bite back a whimper as my skin stings.

Lucas grabs me by my arms, Zephyr grabs my legs, holding me up so I'm floating backwards onto the water. Zephyr bites the inside of my thigh roughly causing my body to jolt.

Lucas responds to my movement by smacking my breast hard making it jiggle. I feel Lucas slide down like he is sitting on the bed of the spring, pulling my body so I'm floating my head on his shoulder.

Zephyr kisses up my thigh moving his body closer, he bites my thigh again, his face just barely away from my dripping pussy. I try to suppress the moan but fail as it echoes through the cave.

"Naughty girl likes it rough it seems Zephyr...maybe we should drive her crazy." Lucas bites my ear a little rough tugging on it causing my body to arch a little.

Zephyr pulls my legs open giving him full access to my pussy and licks me from my clit to my entrance. He slides a finger inside me swirling it around, his tongue going back to my clit moving in circles.

Lucas massages my breasts roughly pinching my nipples hard, he sucks on my neck leaving bites occasionally. My moans are echoing through the cave, I stretch my hands to reach Lucas's dick, I managed to get a good grip on it stroking him slowly.

Zephyr adds 2 more fingers into my core diving his tongue into me as well. The water ripples around us as he adjusts me, so my thighs are resting on his shoulders freeing his other hand. He uses that hand to spread my folds open rubbing my clit furiously.

I feel myself getting close, I stop stroking Lucas as my body trembles. My legs close around Zephyr's head trying to pull him in deeper.

Just when I'm about to explode Zephyr stops and pulls himself away pulling his fingers out swiftly. I whimper at the loss of touch from him.

Lucas stands pulling me with him. He turns me around giving me a small push causing me to falter backwards. Zephyr grabs me from behind pulling me flush against his chest, his dick poking at my ass. I hear a splash of water as Zephyr walks us to the edge of the spring lifting me up.

Lucas pulls me by my arms careful not to actually hurt me and pulls me to a flattened area. Zephyr comes up behind me placing his hands on my hips, his nails digging in. Lucas grabs me by both of my thighs, lifts me up spreading my legs so they go on the side of his hips.

He leans down kissing one side of my neck as Zephyr kisses the other. Both of them slam their dicks inside each of my holes in one fluid motion causing my body to arch against Zephyr's chest.

They keep me tightly pinned there before Lucas pulls himself out of my pussy in a slow drag. He slams back into me in a fast motion then Zephyr does the same thing to my asshole.

They continue going back and forth like this, I'm screaming in pleasure. I feel kisses and bites all over my neck, Zephyr spanks my ass while Lucas pinches and tugs on my nipple.

They both start to move faster matching each other's pace, keeping their rhythm of taking turns in sync. I scream loud as an orgasm shakes my whole body, but they don't stop.

They both continue to pound into me harder and faster, screams and sounds of wet skin slapping against each other echoing through the narrow cave. I feel another orgasm getting close, I also feel the guys dicks twitch as they get close too. My breathing is uneven as I still moan and scream.

They move out of sync to start a new rhythm moving together so they are both going in and out at the same time. My body trembles as a scream echoes through the cave once more when I reach another orgasm, both guys slam as deep as they can into me spilling their seed inside me leaving me feeling very full.

They stay there holding me for a few moments breathing heavy. Lucas pulls out first and unwraps my mouth and eyes. Zephyr pulls out holding onto my waist softer now using one hand to untie my wrists.

I slump into Lucas's arms my body feeling like a limp noodle. Zephyr gathers up everyone's clothes and touches Lucas's arm. Darkness envelopes us as Lucas transports us back to the house and into the bed.

I groan blissfully stretching smiling wide, "Well, that was fun. Give me a little while and I'll be ready again."

Lucas grins as he lays on the bed next to me pulling me onto his chest. "Insatiable," he kisses my head rubbing my back gently, "just the way I love you."

Zephyr lays behind me running a finger up and down my side slowly, "So what made you wake up so horny love?"

I draw circles onto Lucas's chest with my finger, listening to his heart, "we are really hungry, I wanted to work up an appetite."

"Why didn't you tell me, I would've made you some breakfast." Zephyr says giving my ass a smack.

"Not for food, we need blood, fresh blood." I sit up, turn to look at Zephyr, "when you gave us a little bit yesterday it woke up that need for freshness. We haven't had it in so long that it makes it easier for us to get hungrier faster."

Lucas sits up stretching his arms, "Give me a few minutes and I'll bring you a glass sweetheart."

I grab his wrist to stop him from standing up, "no.... from the source is preferred. We discussed it this morning and everyone understands it needs to be done."

Lucas and Zephyr look at each other in a silent communication before Lucas gives him a nod. "Before we allow that, we have something you should know Ivy," Zephyr starts to say.

I turn towards him confused, "ok…"

Zephyr takes a deep breath before he looks me in the eyes, "We are more than willing for you to bite us, however there is a slight complication because it will also start the marking process for fated mates."

I completely freeze unable to breathe or focus, the others inside yell out a collective: WHAT?! My head feels like it's splitting open as they all are trying to take control creating pandemonium in our head.

Lucas gently touches my back, "We both are your fated mates. I knew when I came back and hugged Arachne. That first time touching her ignited the bond in me. I saw that she didn't recognize it, so I felt like not moving too fast was a smarter thing to do."

Zephyr sits in front of me taking my hands, "I felt it when Lilli came into the café, we locked eyes and I touched her hand. The bond snapped into place, but she made it clear she didn't notice. Trix mentioned a fiancé, so I tried to push myself away."

I close my eyes tight as the others get louder. I reach in letting out a scream into the mindscape, they all get thrown into their rooms with the doors slamming shut, I pull the main door shut hard blocking them out. When the pain subsides, I open my eyes looking at Zephyr.

He is waiting for my response concerned, I take a deep shaky breath. "Are you sure?"

He nods stroking my hands, "I'm innately drawn to you. I can anticipate what you need before you even need it. I can see every shift when something is going through you."

Lucas rubs my back, "I can find you in any corner of this earth. When I'm traveling between shadows, usually I need my ears to find the shadow I'm looking for when looking for something specific. When it comes to you I see a bright white light and can be lead to you instead of hunting for the right shadow."

"We are more than willing to allow you to feed on us. We would prefer it and would love to mark you, make you ours. We just had to wait for you to snap out of the fear of the bite to take that step." Zephyr moves his hands to my face stroking my cheek. "I think Lilli needs to be the one to do it though since she was our mate at birth but all of you need to be present together since you share the body."

I nod trembling, "give us a few moments, we will want to talk privately first."

Zephyr kisses my forehead before he gets off the bed, Lucas kisses the back of my head doing the same and they both leave the room shutting the door behind them.

I lay on the bed closing my eyes, retreating into the mindscape.

MINDSCAPE

I walk through the doors and go to my seat at the table. Bellatrix storms through her door, swings a punch towards me but I duck my head just in time but she shatters the back of my chair.

🍃 "What the fuck Trix?!" I yell jumping out of my chair and out of her reach.

She rushes towards me tackling me to the floor pinning me down hard. 🔥 "What the fuck were you thinking?! Why the fuck did you lock us up?!" She starts punching me hard.

Arachne bursts through her door and tries to pull Trix off me. 💧 "Lilli I need help!"

Lilli finally gets through her door, but she sounds a little weak. 🌬 "I don't feel good..."

All our heads snap towards her, she looks paler, dark circles around her eyes, and cheeks a little sunken in. I push Trix off me rushing to Lilli.

Bella walks towards us with Ara in tow, I help Lilli sit down frowning, 🍃 "You need to take over and feed on them. You're starving to the point you will go into a blood rage."

Arachne crouches down in front of Lilli putting her hand on her knee, 💧 "Because this is your body, you are the only one to feel the effects of starvation. Ivy is right...you need to try."

🌬 "I'm scared," Lilli admits her body trembling uncontrollably.

💧 "We will be here with you the whole time Lilli, you're not alone," Arachne stands up grabbing her waist helping her stand. I do the same taking one arm, Bellatrix grabs the other arm.

Together we lead her to the door, letting go. 🔥 *"We will be right here,"* Bellatrix tells her as we stand in front of the door together.

🌬 *Lilliana's POV*

I open my eyes, feel a burning pain in my throat, my fangs ache, there is a pounding in my head in sync with my heartbeat. "Zephyr," I call out.

Zephyr and Lucas come into the room, standing in front of the bed. "Lilliana?" Zephyr asks checking who is in control.

I nod, "Yeah," my voice cracks from the strain of speaking. I rub my throat a little coughing.

Lucas sits next to me while Zephyr sits on the other side, "Are you ready to complete the mate bond with us?" Lucas asks in a soft tone, his hand reaches to stroke my cheek gently.

I don't risk answering, instead I just lean forward and kiss him softly. He kisses me back before taking his shirt off tossing it onto the floor, he does the same to mine before leaning down to kiss my breast.

I look over my shoulder at Zephyr, he leans to me kissing me deeply. He breaks from the kiss pulling his shirt off and standing up so he can take his shorts and boxers off.

Lucas stands up taking his shorts and boxers off as well. He helps me get out of my underwear before crawling back onto the bed laying on his side. He pulls me in front of him stroking my cheek looking in my eyes. "I love you so fucking much Lilli."

"I love you to Lucas," I manage to get out cringing at the pain from talking. Closing my eyes I lean into his touch.

Zephyr crawls into the bed behind me, he kisses my neck, "I also love you Lilliana, we will take care of you until the end of time."

Lucas gives me a deep and passionate kiss caressing my breasts with his hands as Zephyr kisses my neck his hands going down to my legs and spreading them using his own legs to hold mine open. He slides his hand to my core, slips a finger inside while using his thumb to rub my clit.

I reach down to stroke Lucas's dick with one hand while reaching back stroking Zephyr with the other. We stay teasing each other for a little while before Lucas removes his hands from my breasts and moves my hand from his dick. Zephyr moves his hands to my breasts as Lucas angles himself at my entrance.

I continue to stroke Zephyr as Lucas slides himself inside me. I moan into Lucas's mouth softly continuing to kiss him deeply.

Zephyr stops massaging my breast and moves away ruffling in the drawer next to the bed. After a moment he gets back in behind me going back to kissing my neck while massaging my breasts.

He lines himself to my other entrance and slowly slips in. I can tell he lubed himself up, I break from the kiss with Lucas to angle my face towards Zephyr who leans in kissing me softly.

Both of them start to move their hips in time with each other, I moan into Zephyr's mouth. Lucas kisses my neck as they move faster. I break from the kiss breathing heavy moaning loud.

Zephyr moves his mouth to my neck kissing and sucking on it. I feel my orgasm getting closer, I feel a sharp pain on my neck as Lucas sinks his fangs into my neck marking my left side. The pain fades quickly as I feel a small snap in my chest.

Zephyr bites the right side of my neck beginning the marking process there as well, another snap is felt. Moaning in ecstasy I lean forward towards Lucas's neck, biting deeply into him. The blood rushes into my mouth, the bond completely snapping into place with him.

Lust, love, pleasure, pain, sorrow, and longing floods through from the bond. I pull my fangs out moaning as they keep pumping their hips. My orgasm getting closer with each thrust, after a couple more I lose control as I explode with pleasure. Lucas groans as he can feel through the bond how euphoric I'm feeling, he thrusts as deep as possible reaching his own orgasm, Zephyr follows shortly after.

Lucas pulls out of me when Zephyr is finished, goes to the bathroom getting into the shower. Zephyr pulls himself out, gently turns me facing him using my hips. He kisses me softly before angling his head so I can mark him.

I lean down and bite into his neck closing my eyes feeling the bond snap in place as the blood rushes into my mouth. I feed from Zephyr his hands hold my body close trusting me. I lose myself to high of blood, feeling full but I don't want to stop, 🌬️ *it tastes so good.*

Bellatrix speaks up 🔥 *Lilli that's enough, you've got your fill.*

I give a growl in response not letting go of Zephyr's neck lost in the blood rage, my teeth sinking deeper. 💧 *Lilliana! Stop!!* I feel a rush of cold flood through my body making me jolt and release Zephyr.

I sit up quickly wrapping my arms around my knees pulling them close to my chest. Zephyr stays laying there but I can hear his heart still beating.

Chapter 15

Lucas comes into the room, sees me then Zephyr. He sits on the bed lifting my face so he can see my eyes, "Lil are you ok? What's wrong?"

I pull my face away, feeling the rush of hurt come from his side of the bond. The guilt weighs heavily, I get out of the bed going into the bathroom locking the door behind me.

I get into the shower turning it as hot as it'll possibly go. It's not long before I get joined in the shower by Zephyr and Lucas. I turn my backs to them not wanting to see their faces, afraid of what I'll find.

Zephyr sends feeling of love and reassurance through the bond letting me know he's ok. Lucas still has a hint of hurt and worry but he mainly feels undying love. Tears flow down my face as they both wrap me in a tight hug.

After a few minutes letting me cry Lucas releases me, I look up at Zephyr. He smiles brightly, sense of pride and contentment as he locks onto my eyes. "I'm ok princess. You did great. Why did you run from us?"

"I went too far, I lost control...I hurt you." I look at his neck, it has healed leaving my mating mark on his neck. It resembles a bat under a red moon, I reach out touching it softly, Zephyr stiffens as I feel pleasure rush through the bond.

He gives a small laugh leaning down kissing me deeply. *You would never hurt me Lilliana Nightshade. I would never* leave you for something silly like losing control. You are my mate, from now till the day Selene calls us home. I can feel the truth of his words come from the bond, most vampires would be shocked to hear a voice in their head but because I'm used to it, it doesn't faze me when he can.

I love you Zephyr, thank you, I kiss him deeper wrapping my arms around his neck.

He breaks from the kiss, looking into my eyes, "Any time princess." Each of us get out of the shower, drying off and get dressed.

My phone beeps on the table, I grab it and see Sedrick messaged me. "Hey doll, I was wondering if you wanted to have an early birthday dinner with me and Kels? We miss you and want to treat you. Let me know. SM"

Smiling I turn to the guys, "Sedrick wants to have dinner, would you care to join? He wants to celebrate my birthday."

Something sparks through the bond with both of them, but I can't understand what, it fades as quickly as it came. Lucas nods, "Yeah sounds great sweetheart. I'd love to meet the guy in person."

"We can go to Francesco's again, I can have them close the restaurant for us so we can enjoy it," Zephyr says as he grabs his phone making the call.

I text Sedrick back, "Francesco's tonight at 6, that alright with you?" I get a quick response saying ok, setting the phone down I look at the time, it's barely lunch time.

"I feel great, what can we get up to today?" I sit on the edge of the bed smiling at Lucas.

He grins, "Why don't we check out Zephyr's shop? I would like to know where I'm going to be working."

"Sounds like an adventure. Let's do it!" I jump up, grab my phone and backpack.

Lucas laughs, Zephyr gets off the phone joining us. "What's funny?"

I roll my eyes, leaning up to kiss him, "He's laughing at me for being silly. We want to check out your shop and explore, learn more about you my mysterious dragon."

His smile makes my heart flutter as he nods in approval. He grabs his keys to the Cougar, opening the passenger door for me.

"I'm taking the bike," Lucas tells us as he pulls his helmet on.

Zephyr gets in, we drive toward the city. Lucas drives next to the passenger side, when he sees me watching he gives a wave before throttling his bike, popping a wheelie. I laugh, which causes Zephyr to see what I'm seeing.

"Show off," Zephyr mumbles loud enough for me to hear. We pull into a very busy mechanic shop "Volos' Restoration and Repair." Zephyr gets out, walks to my door opening it for me. I take his hand looking around, there are cars in the parking lot filling almost every space.

Lucas pulls up next to me, pulls off his helmet and whistles, "Business looks good."

Zephyr shrugs, "It usually is, I poach mechanics straight out of school or offer jobs to those I see working in their own garage. Only the best of the best here."

I look at him confused, "If business is good, why do you work menial jobs like serving or as a barista?"

"I got bored, I promoted my head mechanic to an assistant manager so I could take a break. I am excited for you to meet him, he is...unique." He leads us inside showing us the lobby. It seems very comfortable and showcases different restorations they have done along the walls.

He leads us to an office in the back opening the blinds to a large window behind the desk. It looks out into the garage portion showing mechanics working on various projects.

He sits at his desk pulling me into his lap, "what do you think princess?"

I look around noticing his office is just as minimalistic as his house. Smiling, I say "Could use some decorating, looks a little bare."

"Well, I never really had someone to help me with that. By all means my love decorate how you see fit." Zephyr says rubbing my back.

Lucas stands by the window looking at the garage lost in thought. We hear a knock on the door, it opens and a 15 year old boy walks in.

He's wearing black coveralls, fiery red hair, blue eyes, and has grease and oil smudged on his hands with some marks on his face. "Mr. Volos, your back!" He smiles big as he approaches the desk.

"Yeah Will, how are things going?" Zephyr strokes my side looking at the kid with a smile, I feel pride radiating through him.

Will sets a pile of papers down on the desk, "Good, we are working on a couple VIP cars and should be done soon. Some of the guys were having trouble with the computer systems the client wanted to add on, but I managed to get them fixed. Sales are up 80%, we have had one accident where oil overflowed. I put a new policy in so that we take a break after lunch to clean the shop before anyone resumes work AND we do a deeper clean after the last car for the day." As he tells Zephyr more of the shop's status I feel that sense of pride and awe get stronger.

I clear my throat causing Will to pause and acknowledge me. "I'm really sorry sir, was I interrupting you?" Will asks timidly.

Zephyr laughs shaking his head, "No kid, this is Lilliana. She's my girlfriend. I wanted to show her and my friend Lucas the garage."

Will blushes, "Nice to meet you ma'am, sir, I apologize for being rude and not introducing myself before. I'm William Fagan."

"Pleasure to meet you Will, how long have you worked here?" I ask walking over to him, holding a hand towards him.

"3 years," he looks at my hand and blushes, "you don't want to shake my hand miss, it's all dirty."

Zephyr chokes back a laugh, "Shake her hand before she pouts Will."

Will gives my hand a small shake being as gentle as possible. "You won't hurt me Will," I smile giving him a good handshake, "you seem like a good kid. How do you work for this mischievous devil?"

"Hey!" Zephyr protests, Lucas laughs finally cracking.

"He's not a devil! Don't call him out of his name again!" Will tells me standing straighter, a dark shade of anger flickers across his eyes.

Zephyr stands up, "William...I'll warn you one time and one time only. Don't...EVER...raise your voice to her again. She is teasing me, and you would do well to remember what we have discussed."

Will blinks a couple times as he backs up taking slow, deep breaths closing his eyes. "Apologies sir," he takes another breath before opening his eyes looking at me, his eyes softer, "I'm sorry for raising my voice Miss Lilliana. I don't like it when people disrespect Mr. Volos. I struggle to understand humor."

I go to him giving him a gentle hug wrapping my arms around him, he stands there stiffly unsure what to do. Leaning down to his ears I whisper, "Nothing to apologize for Will, thank you for caring about him to fight for him."

Will gives me a nod, I release him from the hug with a warm smile. "Why don't you show me around the garage?"

He looks to Zephyr who nods approval, he leads me to the garage showing me around. "Mr. Volos likes to keep things clean and organized, says that an organized workplace makes for less accidents, in other words he doesn't have to pay a client, he gets paid." He points out a couple of the cars in the bays, I see one that looks familiar.

I clear my throat going to the black Charger looking it over, "What can you tell me about this?"

"This is a custom job for a VIP. This is one of my projects I'm working on. They are asking for some intricate alterations to be added that are proving...troublesome even for me. I'm hoping Mr. Volos will help me." He looks over the car, starting to work on it and forgetting about me.

This is Lennix's car, I tell the others, *I can still smell him all over it.*

Bellatrix is fuming, *Set it on fire. He treasures this car, so destroy it!*

No, this is Zephyr's business. We shouldn't do anything to negatively impact him, Arachne counters.

I head back to the office, Zephyr is going through some paperwork while Lucas is filling some out. I sit on the empty chair in front of the desk fidgeting with my fingers.

Zephyr looks up from his stack of papers, "I can feel your anxiety, what's wrong love?"

Lucas has stopped as well, looking at me, I clear my throat. "Will was showing me around the garage and we stopped at a project he has. Black Charger, do you know of it?"

"One second," he flips through some papers to find the order then growls loudly, "Lennix Wolfe."

I nod, as he looks over the form, he seems confused. "What is it?" I ask, my anxiety getting worse.

He stands up, "Come with me." We all go to the garage and asks Will to pop the hood. Lucas looks at the engine, he must notice something because he gets closer.

"Why is the engine so ramped up?" Lucas looks to Will.

"Guy said something about needing to make a quick get-away occasionally and that he has enemies who would like to hunt him down." Will responds tapping on the hood.

🔥 *Yeah he's not wrong about that*, Bellatrix replies.

Ivy laughs, 🍃 *Funny how he thinks making his car faster will help him out run you Trix.*

🌬 *Both of you pipe down...I don't think that's everything. Zeph is concerned, I don't think it's about the speed*, I inform them both.

"Will...did you complete the whole order yet or are you still finishing it?" Zephyr asks as Will gets in the driver's side, hooking a laptop to the car's dash.

"I finished the bulletproofing of the glass, but I'm struggling with the wiring for the security system he wants. I was going to call you at the end of the day to ask for help." Will goes to the passenger seat climbing in, "He wants cameras giving the car a 360 degree view inside and out, locks that are biometric to get in or out of the vehicle, collision or contact warning, and to be able to control the car with his phone instead of having to physically be near it."

◊ *He's building an impenetrable cage*, Arachne informs us.

"Thank you Will, I'm taking over. If he asks though, you did all the work, ok kid?" Zephyr smiles at Will, he smiles back before he nods getting out of the car.

Lucas looks at me worried, I just shake my head, *later...we talk about this later. Too many ears here.* Lucas nods in response and we both look at Zephyr who is typing on the laptop.

"Lucas why don't you and Lil get comfortable in my office, finish filling out your paperwork and order some lunch. I'll be up shortly," Zephyr tells Lucas still zoned in working.

Lucas gently grabs my elbow leading me back to the office. I sit in Zephyr's chair, Lucas goes back to his paperwork. "He's building a cage to try to kidnap me." My voice cracks as I feel the weight of the situation.

"That cage won't hold you sweetheart," Lucas gets up from his chair, crouches down in front of me laying his hands on mine, "have a little more faith in us as a whole."

I look into his eyes, tears threatening to fall, "I've faith in both of you...myself not so much," I admit.

Lucas laughs leaning up kissing me softly, "I've got faith in you, so does Zephyr. That's more than enough I promise."

I nod, stroking his hands in mine. "Let's order something for lunch before Zeph gets crabby."

"Alright babe, what sounds good to you?" He asks pulling out his phone.

"Pizza," I tell him turning to watch the garage.

He places an order and goes back to his paperwork. After about 20 minutes Zephyr comes into the office carrying the pizza order, setting it down on the desk before walking over to me pulling me from the chair and giving me a deep kiss holding me close.

I break from the kiss smiling, "What was that for?"

"I hadn't kissed you for a while, I was going through withdrawals," he winks, sits down in his chair pulling me into his lap, "let's eat lunch then we can talk."

Between the 3 of us the pizza is gone by the time we are done. "So, what's the plan Z?" Lucas asks after cleaning up the mess from lunch.

"I made a couple tweaks that are not noticeable for the biometric coding, I would need both of you to come down and touch the sensor so that I can add you in. I also added a backdoor tracker so that I can monitor where the car is at all times. As for the remote control I made it so that he has limited control, he cannot drive it, all he can do is lock it and monitor the car itself." Zephyr strokes my back offering me comfort as he speaks, "I need to fulfill the order, but I can still make tweaks that are hidden without putting my business at risk."

"Alright, let's do it, then we can talk about your plans for the shop and how you want to expand," I say while standing up from his lap.

We all head to the garage, Zephyr has me put my hand on a thumbprint sensor while adding me to the system. He does the same to Lucas, does some more work on the computer, when he is done he calls Will over handing him the computer showing the bare minimum of what Lennix asked for.

"You can tell the client the car is ready for pickup, I already adjusted the wires and added the cameras as well. You did good kid, I'm proud of you." Zephyr ruffles Wills hair making him blush, but Will has a huge smile on his face.

"Thank you sir, I didn't want to let you down after you promoted me." Will takes the paperwork, does the last bit of invoicing, inputting it into the computer.

The 3 of us head back to the office, Zephyr closes the blind to the garage and sits in his seat while me and Lucas occupy the 2 seats in front.

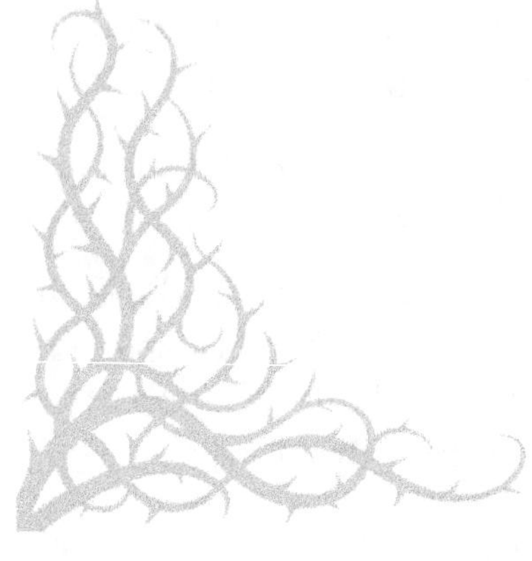

Chapter 16

Lilliana's POV

"I hired a contractor to build a second garage next to this one. It won't be directly connected except by extending the lobby. I need to hire some more bike mechanics to fill up the roster," Zephyr sifts through his desk drawers, pulls out a blueprint laying it out. "I would like you to have full control of the motorcycle side Lucas, you can pick the name for it as well."

Lucas's jaw drops looking at Zephyr, "What? Why me? I don't have any experience running anything let alone a garage."

Zephyr grins, "Because I want you to know you're equal with me, I don't want you to feel like you need to compete or prove yourself. Plus, you spotted the extra horsepower on Lennix's car without even messing with it. I've got guys here who would not have even noticed it without tearing the engine apart."

"Remember how you said I need to have more faith in us as a whole?" I ask Lucas, he nods so I continue, "That means having more faith in yourself. You are smart and quick on your feet. I think you will do just fine Lucas."

He raises a brow at my use of his name then gives in smiling before nodding, "Alright, let's do it."

I pull my book out of my backpack, reading while the 2 of them talk about plans, how Lucas wants the layout, and how he wants to decorate his side of the lobby. Before long they finish. Zephyr gently touches my shoulder, making me put my bookmark in my book in order to look at him.

He smiles brightly, "We are done for today, shall we go to dinner?" I look at the clock, it's 5 o'clock, we have enough time to get back to the house and change before needing to be at the restaurant. I nod, putting my book back in my bag and we head out.

We head to the house, get changed, Zephyr chooses the Jetta to drive back to town. We get to Francesco's, Lucas helps me out of the car. I chose a light cream dress with flats, Lucas chose black jeans and a black button up shirt, Zephyr wore black slacks and dark red button up shirt.

We go inside, sit at the large round table in the middle. I sit between both of the guys as a waiter brings us each a glass of water and a menu. The restaurant is eerily quiet due to being shut down for the night. A few minutes pass before Sedrick and Kelsea join us. I smile wide seeing Sedrick, Kelsea glares at me as I stand up to give Sedrick a hug.

The guys come up behind me, "You must be Sedrick?" Zephyr says holding a hand out for him.

"Yeah," Sedrick releases me from the hug and shakes Zephyrs hand, "Not wanting to be rude but you're not Lennix...so who are you?"

I feel anger from both of the guys as Zephyr has his 'customer service' smile on his face, but Lucas looks pissed, "Zephyr Volos, I'm Lilliana's mate and boyfriend."

Lucas holds his hand out next, when Sedrick looks him over, he smiles, "Lucas I think? I recognize you from the photos Lil would share, she's told me all about you."

Lucas nods shaking his hand, "Lucas Bane, also Lilliana's mate and boyfriend. Nice to finally meet you in person Sedrick."

Sedrick's jaw drops as does Kelsea's, they both look at me in awe. I shrug smiling as Sedrick sees the mating mark on both sides of my neck. "I was blessed with 2 fated mates, and I love them both equally."

Kelsea's eyes darken as she glares at me, giving me a fake smile, "That's wonderful to hear. We should sit down and eat, I don't know about you, but I'm starving."

We all sit down around the table, the waiter comes to take our order and while we wait for the food we talk, "So what happened with Lenny doll?" Sedrick asks.

My lip twitches a little, "We had a falling out, he was being rude and disrespectful. I don't tolerate that." 🔥 *He was also an abusing power-hungry psychopath,* Bellatrix points out.

"That's fair, you deserve better than that. I'm sorry doll I know you guys have been together for a long time, however I'm happy you found your fated mates!" Sedrick smiles brightly.

"If you guys were together for so long, wasn't it worth trying to fix it? Or rejecting your mates for him?" Kelsea asks sipping on her water.

Zephyr speaks before I can, "The mate bond isn't to be tossed aside as if it is nothing. However, when I met Lilli she told me she was engaged so I ignored the bond. When they broke up I took the chance to win her heart." He puts an arm on the back of my chair rubbing my shoulder softly, "She is worth waiting for and she deserves to be treated like the princess she is."

Something flashes in Kelsea's eyes making me look at her curiously, Lucas notices as well but leans closer to me.

Our food comes out and we eat in silence. When we finish eating, the waiter comes to clear the table, Sedrick looks to me, "So how was your birthday dinner doll?"

"It was nice, thank you Sed," I give him a warm smile, "I appreciate you inviting us out. It means a lot to me."

"Any time doll," Sedrick stands holding a hand out to Kelsea, "We need to get going, I just got a mind-link that there is an emergency at home."

We all stand up, I go give Sedrick a hug, he hugs me tight and whispers in my ear, "They better treat you right doll or they will regret it."

I give out a quiet laugh patting his back, "Thank you Sed, I love you bud." I shake Kelsea's hand shivering at the wrongness I feel from her, the two of them leave.

Lucas wraps his arms around my waist from behind kissing his mark on my neck, making me shudder. "Let's go home sweetheart, it's been a long day."

I nod, the 3 of us head back to the car headed home. Somewhere on the way home Zephyr takes a detour going the opposite direction, I look over at him curious, "You're going the wrong way. Change of plans?"

He shakes his head, "We have a tail," Lucas turns to look out the window.

"I don't see anything," Lucas says looking at the stream of cars behind us.

"Rooftop," Zephyr takes my hand pushing the gas pedal further, "it's the same figure I saw the day we met."

Lucas looks up seeing someone running on the rooftops in solid black, "can you try to lose them under a bridge?"

Zephyr shakes his head, he changes direction and heads toward my old apartment. "No, we can leave the car at Lil's old apartment, and you can transport us home. They have teleportation magic, so we won't lose them driving."

He pulls up to the apartment, parks the car, and we all hurry into the apartment locking the door behind us. Lucas grabs both of our wrists sinking us into the shadows. He pulls us out when we get home, wraps me in a tight hug breathing in my scent.

I can feel how nervous Lucas is through the bond, I rub his back softly letting him calm down. "I know it can be scary Shadow, I am fine, we are all fine. I love you." He releases me after a few minutes and yawns covering up his mouth.

Laughing I grab his hand pulling him towards the bedroom, "Come on Zeph, let's go to bed. I think tomorrow should be a stay-at-home day before we face my parents."

Zephyr follows us to the bedroom, the guys strip down to their boxers as I change into one of Lucas's shirts and Zephyrs shorts. I crawl into the center of the bed first, Zephyr lays to my left, Lucas to my right.

I lean in to kiss Lucas softly, "Good night Shadow," I turn, snuggling into Zephyr's arm after kissing him as well, "good night Zephyr." Zephyr holds me close as Lucas curls behind me wrapping his arms around my waist.

I drift to sleep soundlessly.

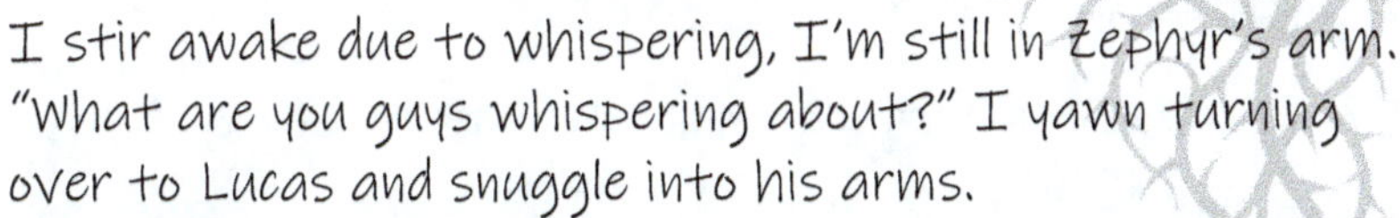

I stir awake due to whispering, I'm still in Zephyr's arm. "What are you guys whispering about?" I yawn turning over to Lucas and snuggle into his arms.

"We were planning a birthday surprise for you babe," Lucas says as he kisses the top of my head holding me close. "We didn't mean to wake you up, go back to sleep."

"No arguments here," I close my eyes drifting back into sleep.

Mindscape

As I stir awake I slip into my mindscape. I go through the doors and sit at the table relaxing. Bellatrix comes through her door, sits at the table, her neck showing the same marks as mine does.

"It burned like a bitch, but good news is they didn't die!" Bellatrix laughs looking at me, "Now we just need to get rid of Lennix and keep our parents away from us then we will have a happy life."

Ivy exits her room, sitting on her chair stretching, "Why do I feel so..." she considers her words trying to find the right one.

"Free?" I throw out, feeling the same way. She nods smiling, "Because we are. Free to be ourselves without fear, free to love who we want, and free to do what we wish."

"Freedom may not be the right word, however I'll agree I do feel more liberated," Arachne says as she joins us at the table.

Ivy flexes her fingers watching them as if feeling something, "I feel different, I can't put my finger on it though."

Bellatrix snaps her fingers, a small flame appearing above her fingers floating, her eyes bright red flickering like the flame before her. "Magic, I noticed I can feel magic like my dream after we completed the mating process. It's like it got unlocked."

I close my eyes thinking, I feel a slight breeze which is odd, I lean into it feeling the rush of air get stronger.

"Um...Lil...are you trying to do that?" Ivy asks in a soft tone.

Opening my eyes I see I'm floating above the chair on top of a cloud. "What the hell is this?!" My anxiety makes the cloud disappear and I crash back into my chair.

Trix laughs, "You control wind it looks like, makes sense since your more adaptable and sociable then us. You need to keep calm and not let fear take over."

Arachne closes her eyes, sits back in her chair, before long we see water flowing up her body encasing her. When she opens her eyes they are both bright blue glowing faintly. She looks to Ivy and nods her head slightly. Ivy frowns taking a deep breath before following suit to close her eyes. I relax floating while watching Ivy, waiting to see what happens.

We all watch Ivy as the wooden chair behind her seems to grow vines wrapping around her body framing each curve perfectly. The vines break from the chair as she opens her eyes, they glow a vibrant green, she looks at her arm smiling. The vine seems to respond to her joy growing a small white rose in her palm.

"All of your eyes are glowing brighter when you use your magic," I tell them smiling. They look at me grinning big.

"So do yours Lilliana, you also seem to have a reaction when we are all using them together," Arachne says after lowering the water to her shoulders.

I float to my room, open the door looking into the mirror, my eyes are indeed glowing bright red and bright green. My marks on my neck glow shifting like a rainbow between red, blue, green, and silver.

I head back to the table, looking at their necks closer, Bellatrix's marks have a red sheen to them, Arachne's are blue, and Ivy's are green. I laugh a little lowering myself into my chair, "We each have our own color. I seem to have a mix of them all, we should practice mastering these gifts."

"Why don't we take turns today?" Arachne suggests, releasing her hold on her water making it disappear, her mark on her neck going back to normal, showing a dragon with silver eyes on her right, and a bat sitting on the shoulders of a wolf on her left.

I shrug nodding, "I don't see why not, I told the guys I wanted to stay home today anyways."

"Oooh can I get first try please?" Ivy jumps up from her chair giggling making the rest of us look at her bewildered.

"You're awfully chipper Ivy...what are you planning?" I ask her skeptically.

She frowns, "I'm not planning anything, I just want to play in the woods. I feel really good and free...I would like to experience that a little more."

Arachne holds up her finger interjecting, "She has been behaving so maybe letting her loose will keep her that way."

"Fine but we need to keep the door open so we can see what we can all do, no blocking," I yell out as she runs to the door.

"Got it!!" She bursts through the door laughing.

"We might regret this," Bellatrix voices as she sits looking at the screen on the table seeing through Ivy's eyes.

Chapter 17

I open my eyes and stretch, Lucas is still sleeping holding onto me. I poke his chest a couple times causing him to stir, "Wake up sleepyhead."

"Go back to sleep Lil," he tugs me closer yawning.

"Not Lilli," I tell him as I pull out of his arms crawling off the bed. I hear clattering in the kitchen, I go to the kitchen seeing Zephyr getting things together for breakfast. Smiling I hop onto the counter next to him and the stove, "Whatcha doin handsome?"

"Making breakfast for you beautiful," he stands in front of me, kisses me softly. I nip his lip when he pulls away which causes him to raise a brow at me.

I give him a wink, "What are you making?"

Lucas comes into the kitchen sits on the barstool by the island, "I think pancakes sound good."

Zephyr nods, he starts making the pancake mix occasionally watching me. He makes a couple stacks of pancakes putting them on the island. "Anything else before we start to eat?"

"I would like some strawberries please," I swing myself off the counter and sit in one of the stools next to Lucas.

Zephyr grabs some strawberries, syrup, and whip cream from the fridge setting them down next to the pancakes. I help myself first, cutting my strawberries into thin slices laying them on my pancakes.

We eat in silence, Zephyr cleans up the plates, I grab the whip cream spraying some in my mouth. Lucas watches me with a grin. "Sweet tooth today huh?"

"Nope, just want a little sugar rush. If I really had a craving I would cover you and Z with it and lick it clean," I grin back at him with a wink putting the whipped cream back in the fridge. The guys watch me with a heated gaze as I go out the backdoor.

I head to the forest finding a grass covered area, *this looks like a good place to try,* I tell the others going to the center. I take a deep breath searching for the magic inside me, I close my eyes letting instinct take over.

Crouching down I stroke the grass keeping my eyes closed and breath even. Vines grow along my hands from the grass, I open my eyes watching as they wrap around my arm slowly like a snake. *It worked!* I can feel the others watching as I let the vines roam all over my body.

What can you do with it other than make vines grow? Bellatrix asks with a sassy tone.

I give a huff, standing up. I form the vine into my hand and lash it out like a whip, a loud crack is heard as it strikes the air. I hear footsteps coming toward me, so I snap the whip in that direction striking a tree branch cutting through it, right next to Zephyr and Lucas barely missing them.

"Oops, sorry guys," smiling sheepishly at them, "got a little carried away."

Lucas walks towards me slowly and warily like I'm going to bolt if he moves too fast, "Lilli are you ok?"

Rolling my eyes I turn my back to them, the vine whip wrapping back around my body snug. "Yes I'm fine, however wrong person Lucas." I look at the bare grass and tilt my head, *I think it would look better with some color,* I hold my hands out palm down and take a deep breath.

Different colored wildflowers start to bloom from the grass turning it into a beautiful meadow. I smile pleased with it before turning back to the guys.

Their mouths are open watching everything unfold. Zephyr shakes his head, clears his throat, "So that's a new development love." He walks to me, giving me a soft kiss.

I wrap my arms around his neck, biting his bottom lip, "Indeed it's, we aren't done yet though." I give him a deep kiss pulling him closer by his neck.

We make out for a bit before he pulls from the kiss laughing softly, "What do you mean by that Ivy?"

"Stick around and find out," I nip his chin backing away closing my eyes. I retreat into the Mindscape to allow someone else to take over.

Bellatrix's POV

I crack my neck, opening my eyes looking at Zephyr. "We are rotating so bear with us," I tell him rubbing my palms together.

He nods, goes back to where Lucas is, sits at the base of the tree watching me. Lucas sits down leaning forward obviously intrigued. "Show us what you got sweetheart,"

Lucas says folding his hands under his chin leaning his elbows on his knees.

I turn to the field Ivy grew grinning, 🔥 *Sorry Ivy but flowers are gonna die*. I hear a string of curses come from Ivy. I let out a laugh snapping my fingers creating a flame above them. Watching the flames on my fingers I try to blow it out.

What I don't expect is that instead of extinguishing, they flare out like dragon breath burning the field and trees in front of me. "Oops...too much," I hold my hand out willing the fire to retreat back to me, they rush into my palm, I can't help but smile. 🔥 *Just like my dream*, I snap my fingers creating the flame again.

Flicking my wrist the flame shoots into the bark of the tree in front of me like a bullet and goes out at impact. I turn to look at the guys seeing Lucas trying to hold back a laugh.

"What's so funny Shadow?" I ask folding my arms daring him to laugh at me more.

He shakes his head, "Nothing at all babe," he tries to compose himself still trying to contain the laugh.

I kick at the grass; a bolt of flame goes straight towards Lucas disappearing in front of his face before contact. "Don't lie to me," I warn him tapping my fingers on my arm.

Lucas blinks taking a slow breath, "You're a force to be reckoned with, I find it funny that no one knew about you before. I wonder what the look on Lennix's face when he sees you burn his dick off will look like."

I tilt my head thinking then can't help but laugh at the idea of it. "Ok that's fair to laugh about," I uncross my arms relaxing. I turn back toward the field stretching my arms.

Alright Arachne, you're up, I close my eyes going back into the mindscape letting her switch.

Arachne's POV

Well...mine is going to be a little tougher to use offensively, I open my eyes wondering what I'm able to do.

Let your instinct guide you, the magic knows what to do, Ivy says trying to offer support.

I nod, clearing my head of the worries I carry. As I feel the burden clear, I can feel the magic tug in my chest. I feel water start to form in my hands, I take a slow breath as the water creeps up my arms feeling cool along my skin.

The calmer I get, the more the water covers my body. As it fully envelopes my body covering my face I turn towards Zephyr and Lucas. *I want to try something, I need you to hurt me*, I tell the both of them through the bond.

Zephyr frowns shaking his head, "I don't want to risk it."

Lucas stands up anyways, "Are you sure sweetheart? What if you actually get hurt?"

Trust me please, I'll be fine, I tell them both standing still keeping the water covering my whole body.

Zephyr stands slowly, taking a deep breath before nodding. He charges at me head on, but I move to the side quickly making him go past me. Lucas tries to tackle me but there is a loud splash as he collides into my water form creating a puddle of water where I stood.

The water moves away from them, I slowly raise from the puddle watching them. Lucas walks over to me, he swings a punch at my arm but is stopped by the wall of water covering me.

The water wraps around his hand holding it in place, he tries to pull but can't get free. "I could use a little help here Zeph," Lucas calls out. Zephyr comes up behind me, clearing his throat before blowing steam from his mouth.

I can feel the water heat up and bubble in response to the heat, but it stays strong. I take a deep breath, will the water to push away from my body. A large rush of water forces both of them to fall backwards onto their backs letting out a grunt from the impact.

I crouch down next to Lucas's head touching his cheek gently. "Are you ok?" I ask softly.

He nods his head letting out a small cough, "Yup, ego is a little bruised, but my body otherwise is fine." He laughs looking up at me.

I give him a soft kiss helping him stand up. Zephyr groans as he sits up, "Well...I think it's safe to say we didn't harm you. The same can't be said the other way around though," he stands up stretching groaning as he pops his back.

"Sorry, I didn't realize it would push you that hard." I walk to him giving him a gentle hug trying to be tender.

He kisses the top of my head hugging me back, "It's absolutely fine love, I was more worried about hurting you."

"It's Lilli's turn," I say as I pull away from the hug letting her take over.

⇌ Lilliana's POV

Zephyr looks at me with a smile, I return the smile before taking his hand. Lucas wraps an arm around my waist kissing my head. "Hold on tight," I warn them both before we all start to float into the air. Air swirls under my feet the higher we go, Lucas grips me tighter, fear radiates down from him.

Zephyr watches as we float higher and higher, laughing in awe. He loosens his hold on my hand when we get high enough, he gives me a wink letting go completely, shifting into his dragon form flying next to me and Lucas.

Lucas clings even tighter, "Please don't let me fall!"

Zephyr moves underneath me and Lucas, *tell him to climb onto my back love, I'll take him back to the ground.*

I pass the message on, Lucas drops onto Zephyrs back, they fly back to the ground. Zephyr shifts after Lucas climbs off hunching over and dry heaving. Zephyr pats his back as I stay in the air looking at the city from afar. ⇌ *It's beautiful up here,* I say to the other girls.

I float back down to the ground smiling ear to ear, Lucas still looks a little pale, but Zephyr walks over to me smiling. "You feel different, stronger more...confident in yourself." Zephyr says taking my face into his hands so he can look into my eyes.

I nod in agreement, "We feel different. I'm getting hungry, we have been out here for so long we skipped lunch." I laugh tiptoeing up so I can kiss him.

Can I fix my meadow first please? Ivy asks giving a little tug trying to get control.

Bellatrix grumbles, *Its too colorful.*

The two of them bicker before I cut in shutting them both up, *knock it off both of you, Trix stop being a bitch to Ivy, Ivy stop whining in order to get your way, yes you may take over.* I retreat into the Mindscape allowing her to take control.

Ivy's POV

I push Zephyr away gently, touching the grass getting the meadow back how I had it. The tree Bellatrix burned also goes back to the way it was, the leaves a little brighter.

I take Zephyr's hand pulling him towards the house, grabbing Lucas's hand as we get near him. When we get into the house Zephyr goes into the kitchen to start on dinner. Me and Lucas go to the living room to sit on the couch together.

"So...each of you have your own gift?" Lucas asks laying an arm on the back of the couch behind me gently stroking my shoulder.

I nod smiling, "I control nature, Ara controls water, Trix has fire, and Lil has air." I hold my palm out, take a deep breath, a small white rose forms into my palm.

Zephyr comes into the living room hearing me, "Sounds fitting if you ask me. Dinner is in the oven should be ready in about an hour." He sits on his loveseat looking at the rose in my hand.

"What do you mean by that?" I ask making the rose disappear.

Zephyr chuckles before answering, "Don't let Trix barbecue me for this, you are wild and free spirited, just like nature. Trix is hotheaded and impulsive, more about destroy now ask questions later. Arachne is more fluid, composed, and prefers to think things through first."

"What about Lil?" I ask tilting my head to look at him.

He smiles, "She craved freedom for so long she needed a way to escape. What better way than to use air? She's more open-minded then the 3 of you as well as sensitive to other emotions."

🔥 *Well, I mean he's not wrong,* Bellatrix says chuckling a little, *he is safe from turning to ash for now.*

"Bella says your safe for now," I lay my head back against Lucas's arm, looking at the ceiling.

Lucas leans forward kissing his mark on my neck causing a shiver to run down my body. I sit back up, push him into the corner of the couch straddling his lap. He moves his hands to my waist grinning up at me, "What's wrong sweetheart? Getting a little hot?"

🌬 *I'm not watching this,* Lilli says, and I can feel her close herself off in her room.

Bellatrix laughs pulling the main door shut to close me off completely.

"Shut up and kiss me doofus," I rip his shirt off before kissing him deeply my hands resting on his chest.

He grabs a handful of my hair roughly kissing me back his tongue dominating mine. I hear Zephyr moving but keep my focus on Lucas. Running my hands down his chest I undo his pants, biting his lower lip as I break from the kiss.

His eyes are dark with lust wanting more, he grabs my shirt ripping it down the middle and pushes himself up causing me to sit back. He pushes me into the other side of the couch caging me in his arms, he bites his mark roughly. A moan escapes as I arch my body towards him. I push his pants down, his erection springs free.

He lifts himself up enough to grab the shorts I'm wearing and rips them to shreds along with my underwear. His mouth slams to mine pinning me against the couch hard. He grabs my legs pulling them up to his hips, he breaks from the kiss and bites my neck as he slams his dick inside my pussy hard. I let out a moan arching my body towards his.

He sinks his fangs into my neck feeding as he moves his hip thrusting into me hard each time he pulls himself out. He feeds his fill licking my neck sealing the bite closed, his mouth finds mine kissing me deeply biting my lip.

He continues his thrusting going faster and harder, my hands grip his back digging my nails in causing him to hiss in pain. I break from the kiss feeling my orgasm getting close, I sink my fangs into his neck over my mark. The rush of blood sending me over the edge as I come all over his dick. He slows to a stop letting me ride out my high.

I release his neck, the high from my orgasm calming down. I lick the bite closing it up breathing heavy. Lucas pulls himself out, grabs my hips lifting me up and flipping me over, so I'm leaning over the edge of the couch, my knees propping me up on the cushion.

Zephyr is standing in front of me stroking his dick with a grin, "Don't think for a second I wasn't joining the party." He moves closer his dick inches away from my face.

I wink opening my mouth for him, he grabs the top of my head his fingers gripping my hair tight. Lucas slams his dick back into my pussy causing me to push my mouth onto Zephyrs dick shoving him all the way to the back of my throat.

Lucas pumps in and out of me hard and fast, each movement making Zephyr's dick go in and out of my mouth. Zephyr's head lays back gripping my hair tighter, I use one of my hands to caress his balls. Lucas starts to thrust harder, I can feel his dick twitch as he gets close to his finish.

My orgasm builds as they keep going, Lucas smacks my ass hard causing my body to jolt. My moan muffled by Zephyrs dick, Lucas moves faster. He spanks me again before moving his hand to the front of my leg rubbing my clit hard with his fingers.

Zephyr spills out in the back of my throat holding my head there as I swallow all of it. Lucas moves his fingers faster on my clit, I come again as Lucas thrusts deep inside filling my pussy with his seed. Zephyr pulls his dick from my mouth releasing my hair, walks to the kitchen and comes back with a warm rag cleaning his dick off before tossing it to Lucas.

Lucas pulls his dick out of me wiping himself off before wiping me clean helping me sit back down against the couch. He pulls his pants and boxers back up before he sits down next to me taking a deep breath.

Zephyr pulls his pants back on, goes to the bedroom before bringing me a pair of shorts and t-shirt. I take them from him putting them on stretching as I move.

Zephyr hears a ding in the kitchen, "Perfect timing, dinner is ready." He goes to the kitchen, me and Lucas go to the dining table.

Zephyr brings a baking dish, setting it on the table, *He made lasagna...from scratch,* I lean closer grinning. I grab the spatula cutting a big slice putting it on my plate.

Zephyr laughs getting himself a slice and serves one to Lucas. We eat quietly, when I finish what I put on my plate I get seconds.

Between the 3 of us we devour the whole lasagna. I lean back in my chair feeling full. "That was delicious Zeph," I say patting my full belly.

"Dude that was the best lasagna I ever had," Lucas groans as he stretches leaning back.

Zephyr smiles proud of himself, "Thanks, I'm glad you guys liked it." He cleans the table off, I get up to help him wash the dishes. Lucas dries them with a towel as I hand them to him.

When we are finished Lucas tosses the towel at my face with a grin. "I'm going to hop in the shower before bed," Lucas says walking away to the bedroom.

Zephyr comes up behind me, kisses his mark wrapping his arms around me softly. He rests his chin on my shoulder, we stay like that for a few minutes before he talks, "How are you feeling Ivy?"

I smile rubbing his arm, "Complete."

"I understand that feeling," he says hugging me tighter, "I'm happy that Lilli came to the café, I've looked for a mate for a very long time. Little did I know that I would have 4 wonderful women to drive crazy."

Laughing I turn around in his arms wrapping my arms around his neck, "We were already crazy, you just enhance it a little."

"Fair enough," he kisses my forehead as he picks me up sweeping my legs under his arms. He carries me to our room, Lucas is lounging on the bed wearing clean boxers, his hair still a little wet and playing on his phone.

He sets me down on my feet. I go into the bathroom to start a warm bath, Zephyr follows me in but hops into the shower. When the bath fills I step in relaxing in the hot water.

I close my eyes, laying my head back feeling the water sooth my muscles. I hear the shower door creak as Zephyr gets out, I hear the towel ruffle as he dries himself off, he kisses the top of my head before going to the bedroom shutting the door behind him.

when the water starts to get cold I unclog the drain, get out wrapping a towel around my body. Heading into the bedroom I see the guys relaxing on the bed messing with their phones. I drop the towel crawling into bed between the two of them.

Lucas sees me and grins putting his phone down laying next to me, "Not satisfied love?"

"I'm plenty satisfied," I yawn flexing my arms and legs before snuggling into Lucas's arm, drifting to sleep.

Chapter 18

Ivy's POV

I wake with a start feeling like something is off. Lucas stirs opening his eyes, "You ok love?"

I shake my head trembling. He sits up wrapping his arms around me tight, "Breathe Ivy, you're here safe with us."

Zephyr wakes hearing Lucas calm me down and frowns sitting up, "What's going on?"

"I don't know Z, she won't stop shaking," Lucas answers rubbing my arms, "it's ok Ivy, you probably had a bad dream."

I shake my head quickly, sinking into the mindscape running to Lilli's door knocking frantically.

Mindscape

Lilli doesn't answer, I try to open the door, but it doesn't budge. "Ara! Trix! Help me!" I yell out banging on Lilli's door harder.

Bellatrix comes running out of her room, "I feel it too," she slams her body into the door hard but bounces off.

"LILLIANA OPEN THE DOOR!" I scream kicking and punching the door.

Arachne comes out of her room pulling me away from the door, ◊ "Knock it off, you know the rules. We can't force ourselves into another's room."

Bellatrix shoves Arachne off of me, 🔥 "We can't fucking feel her Ara. Get your head out of your ass and help us get in there."

Bellatrix puts her hand on the door closing her eyes, Arachne blinks slowly realizing why we are frantic as she feels the same. Ara stands next to Trix putting her hand on the door closing her eyes too.

I do the same thing, the 3 of us concentrating on the door. Slowly the door disintegrates in our hands, our eyes snap open and we see Lilli laying on her bed eyes wide open staring at the ceiling her eyes glowing faintly.

We each get inside the door standing next to the bed, I lean down and press a hand to Lilli's cheek, 🍃 "Lilli, wake up," I gently call out, but she doesn't respond.

Bella puts her hand in Lilli's holding it firmly, 🔥 "Lilliana, come back to us."

Arachne looks Lilli over, she puts her hand above Lilli's heart, ◊ "We are here Lil, you're not alone."

A shadow cover's Lilliana's body, the color in her eyes begin to fade. I look to Ara tears falling, 🍃 "What's happening to her?"

◊ "I don't know, we need help. Bella take control, tell the guys to send everything they have through the bond, we need to give her everything." Ara tells Trix. Bellatrix nods letting go of Lilliana's hand rushing out of the room.

I look at Lucas frowning, "Something's wrong with Lilli, we are losing her. We need help."

Lucas and Zephyr tense, Zephyr takes my hand, "What do you need?"

"Flood the bond, call out to her, send all your love, fear, everything. We are doing the best we can, but we don't know what's happening." I take Lucas's hand in my free one. "We are scared," I admit closing my eyes.

They both squeeze my hand, "There's something I should tell you. It's about your parents," Lucas says his voice shaky.

Turning to look at him I frown, "I don't think now is the time for this Lucas."

"They put a curse on Lilliana when she was born. They said something about her 25th birthday making it crucial she stays near Lennix." Lucas tells me quickly, I barely get the chance to respond when Ara screams at me to hurry.

"We can talk about it later, flood the bond!" I grip their hands tight going back into the Mindscape.

I run into Lilli's room, Ara is pressing on Lilliana's chest water flowing from her fingers. Ivy is holding Lilli's head a swarm of lilies all over the bed. Understanding what they are doing I go back to where I stood before taking

Lilli's hand, my hand is covered in flames as it wraps around hers tying us together.

We hear the guy's voices carry through the bond calling for Lilliana. The shadow over Lilli begins to fade, I start to whisper her name. Her eyes start to brighten, Ara and Ivy see this, so they whisper her name in tune with me. The more we call to her the more her eyes start to glow.

When the shadow disappears, she jolts to a sitting position quickly throwing her arms around my neck tight. I let out a relieved sigh wrapping my arms around her tight, Ara joins in the hug, then Ivy.

A bright light explodes around us causing us to close our eyes tight.

The light dies down, we open our eyes pulling away from each other. Lilliana has tears flowing down her face, but she has a smile.

"You guys got rid of the darkness, thank you," she wipes her face pulling us back in for a quick hug.

I hug her back before pulling away, "Lucas knows what happened, we need to find out what he knows." I tell them, I'm pissed because Lucas kept a secret. My eyes are on fire as I go to the main door taking control.

I look at Lucas and Zephyr holding my hands in theirs. I push them both away getting out of the bed. "Explain what you know about the curse. NOW!" My arms light up in flames, I cross them on my chest standing away from both of them.

Zephyr looks to Lucas before he sits on the end of the bed looking at me, "The day Lilli had a meltdown because we urged her to feed, Lucas went to find out what was going on. He listened in on Julian hoping to find some clues."

Lucas sits next to Zephyr rubbing his hand anxiously, "They talked about a curse they placed on Lilli when she was born. How it was supposed to keep her weak and docile. A witch, Chelsea, was the one to put the curse on her." He tenses up as he continues, "Chelsea admitted that the curse was weakening but unsure of the cause. Lennix informed her that me and Z were following you around at that point."

"She figured out that one of us were your mates, she said that triggering the mate bond weakened the magic. They hoped to stop us from completing the mate bond because it would rid the curse completely," Zephyr takes over the explanation, "Chelsea has a minion working for her. Whether he knows or not is unclear, but she has him doing whatever he asks."

Lucas frowns looking into his palm, "She has Sedrick. She inserted herself in Sedrick's life for the sole purpose to get close to Lilli hoping to fix the problem."

I growl loudly surprising both of the guys making their head snap up to me seeing my hair on fire as I get angrier, "Kelsea. I knew there was something off about her when I met her."

Zephyr nods his head, "She's the one who attacked you that night. She ran before I could catch her."

My arms drop to my side, I pace back and forth in front of the back door. *It's fucking insane. What the fuck are we a part of?*

I don't know, but I want to kill the bitch. She used our friend to get close to us, Lilli says, I can feel her temper rise.

"Our parents...cursed us. Our best friend's girlfriend is the witch to do it. Our ex-fiancé was in on the plan, and our fated mates kept this secret from us when it could've helped prevent this meltdown." I close my eyes taking a deep slow breath, as I let it out I open my eyes, the flames in my hair and my arms dying out. "I need air."

Going to the closet I change into jeans and a T-shirt, slip on my sneakers and go out through the back door. The guys start to follow me but I stop them, holding my hand up, "Don't even think about it. If you come near me right now I'll fucking turn you to ash." My hand covers itself in flames causing them to freeze on the spot.

I feel hurt, rejection, and guilt flood from them. Shaking my head I walk off leaving them at the house.

Zephyr's POV

"We fucked up," I tell Lucas as I walk to the kitchen.

"I know," Lucas says walking behind me. He sits at the island covering his face with his hands. "How do we fix it?"

I grab a glass of water and sit next to Lucas, "Well...it's her birthday, so why don't we take her to get pampered before we go to the ball? Maybe even give her a birthday present to show we won't leave?"

"I have a bad feeling about the ball, it feels like a trap to cage Lil. What if they try to take her?" Lucas asks lowering his hands.

I shrug, "Then we kill them. No one touches our princess. Simple as that."

He nods, "I need a smoke."

We get up to go outside to the deck, he pulls out his cigarettes and lights one up taking a long drag. He sets the pack on the table between us, and I grab one lighting it up as well. He looks at me curious before looking back in the direction Trix walked off.

We sit in silence waiting for her to return. It felt like hours passed before she finally did.

Lilliana's POV

I see the guys on the back porch smoking, walking up to them I cross my arms holding them close to my chest. "I'm sorry she walked off, we needed to calm down." I tell them standing a few feet away.

Zephyr shakes his head tossing his finished cigarette into the gravel, "Don't apologize princess, we screwed up. We should've told you."

"Yeah, you're right about that. But it's over with now, I don't want to spend the rest of today angry." I watch as they both relax a little more, "You really hurt us. Don't keep secrets from us again."

Lucas stands holding a hand out, "I swear on my life, we won't."

I step closer and take his hand gently, Zephyr stands holding his hand out. "No more secrets, I'm deeply sorry I hurt you princess, it was not intentional," he says frowning slightly.

I take his hand moving closer. They wrap their other arms around me hugging me close between them. I take a shaky breath and clear my throat. "So, what's the plan today? I know we planned to go to the ball but I'm not sure if that's wise knowing my parent's cursed me and manipulated me my whole life."

Zephyr pulls away letting go of my hand stroking my cheek, "We actually were thinking of still going. Maybe you can still enjoy the dance with us, we figured we could take you to get your nails, hair, make-up done and show up united and happy. It would definitely cause some feathers to be ruffled."

"Plus, we don't want those outfits to go to waste do we? Lisa busted her ass to get them done in one day. I would love to see the look on Julian's face when he sees you are a strong bad-ass princess with 2 ferocious mates," Lucas says smiling.

What do you guys think? Ball? I ask the others.

Arachne answers first, *I feel like it might be fueling the fire. Too risky.*

We can handle the fire, lets kick some ass, Bellatrix says.

Ivy hums softly before she gives her input, *I think we should go. The guys will protect us.*

I look to the guys and nod, "Let's do it."

Zephyr smiles leading me back into the house, I drag Lucas with us. Zephyr grabs all 3 garment bags with our outfits laying them on his arms, we go to the Cougar, and he lays them in the trunk.

We drive to the city arriving at a nail salon. I go to the counter, they do a manicure and pedicure. I chose to do a coffin style acrylic with black gel and silver stones for my hands, and a simple black gel for my feet.

When they finish drying I head to the guys. We walk next door to the hair salon, I get my hair trimmed and styled with some curls. Lucas and Zephyr get their hair trimmed, Zephyr gets his beard trimmed. When we finish Lucas plays with my curls, "Getting hungry for lunch sweetheart?" He asks releasing my hair.

"I could eat," I admit smiling softly. I feel more relaxed than before.

We head to a little diner, sit down and order lunch. When we finish I stretch my arms, Zephyr uses the opportunity to slide closer to me to kiss me softly. I giggle kissing him back wrapping my arm around his neck. "Smooth," I say breaking from the kiss.

"Let's get your makeup done and then make one more stop. I rented a hotel room close to the venue so we can change there.

I nod, he pays for the food, and we head out. When we get back to the car Lucas gently presses me against the door kissing me deeply. When he breaks from the kiss he smiles, "Your hair looks great when its straight, but looks phenomenal when they have curls."

"Thank you Shadow," I give him a quick kiss getting into the car.

We drive to a make-up shop, the guys watch as a young lady does my face make-up keeping it minimal. She hands me a lip-gloss container after we are finished, Zephyr and Lucas both are staring at me in awe. I look in the mirror and smile, she put black eyeliner, black eye shadow, and silver gemstones on the corner of my eye. My lips are black with silver specks over them with a shiny clear lip-gloss coating it.

"Lilli...you look stunning." Zephyr says holding an arm out.

Looping my arm through his we walk out, "Wait till you see it all together."

We drive for a little while before we arrive in front of a jewelry store. I look at Zephyr confused, but he just smiles getting out of the car. I look at Lucas who shrugs but has a grin telling me he knows something.

We get out, go into the store and an old man approaches us. "Hello, what may I help you with today?"

Zephyr clears his throat, "My girlfriend here would like to get some jewelry for an event tonight. She can tell you what she likes. Me and my friend here are going to look around while we wait for her to decide.

I blush, the guys walk off leaving me with the jeweler. He helps me get the necklace, earrings and bracelet that I feel will accentuate the dress.

The guys join me after the jeweler rings up what I picked out, Lucas pays for it and leads me to the car carrying the bag for me. Zephyr follows a few minutes later.

We get into the car heading to the hotel, "Let me get us checked in, why don't you go next door get some shoes for the ball?" Zephyr suggests grabbing our stuff from the trunk.

"Sure, see you in a few Z," Lucas says grabbing my hand pulling me towards the shoe emporium.

"I'm done shopping," I groan following him. He laughs pulling me close. I head to the heel section to look for some shoes that look good with the vision in my head.

I find a pair of black 3 inch heels with diamond looking stones that would shoe off my pedicure and frame my ankle nicely.

Lucas leads me to the men's section, he finds himself a set of black dress shoes. He pays for them, and we head back to the hotel.

Zephyr is waiting in the lobby, when he sees us coming he smiles brightly. We get in the elevator, Zephyr steps behind me resting his hands on my shoulder. "I know we screwed up, but do you trust me?"

"You may have hurt my feelings, but you didn't break my trust. I understand why you guys kept it from us, I just wish we knew so we were better prepared." I lean back towards him.

He pulls a blindfold from his pocket and gently ties it around my face, "Can you see anything? He asks holding my shoulders.

I shake my head feeling a little nervous now.

Chapter 19

Lilliana's POV

The elevators door opens, he walks me forward. He warns me when there is a step up or down as he leads me towards something. He lets go brushing past me as he walks away.

"Alright princess, take the blindfold off," he tells me. I do as he says blinking to adjust to the light. He and Lucas are kneeling in front of me, each holding a ring.

Oh shit, we all say collectively. My heart hammers in my chest looking at them both frantically.

Lucas speaks first, "Lilliana, Ivy, Bellatrix, and Arachne. I've known you for so long that you felt like home before I learned we were mates. I love how each one of you shine in your own special way. I vow to never leave your side, love you unconditionally, and put my own ambitions and dreams second to yours."

"I've lived a long time, I've been lonely for so long I gave up on the idea of finding my fated mate. Seeing you walk into the café and getting a glimpse into those beautiful eyes I knew I would never be alone again. I would burn this world to ash if it made you happy. Normally I hate the idea of sharing, but with you it doesn't faze me. You treat both of us equally, love us unconditionally, and steal our breath every time you smile, forever is a long time, but you are OUR forever baby," he smiles up at me.

"Will you marry us?" They ask in unison.

SAY YES! The others scream into my head, I nod my head, "Of course I will." They look at each other and laugh, Lucas slides his ring on first, it's a curved silver band with a black diamond on the top. Zephyr slides his on, it's curved gold band with a ruby. When they are both together the stones sit side by side due to the curvature and setting.

I stroke the rings gently, they both get up and Zephyr kisses me deeply picking me up. He breaks from the kiss setting me down with a little laugh, "You make us very happy saying yes."

"It was a collective yes," I turn to Lucas. He pulls me by my waist bending me over kissing me passionately.

I break from the kiss, as he stands me back up, "You're going to mess up my make-up. Behave." He laughs shaking his head.

"I don't think I will," Lucas pulls my clothes off tossing them onto the floor kissing his mark on my neck. Lighting a fire in my core making me press my thighs together in order to smother it.

Zephyr comes up behind me, kisses his mark as he grabs my hands pulling them above my head holding them up, "Don't move your hands princess," he whispers into my ear.

Clearing my throat I nod, keeping my hands up in the air. He trails his fingers slowly down my arm, barely touching my skin. I feel like heat is running down my arms as he trails his fingers lower. He glides down my side making me shiver, Lucas unbuttons my pants leaning down taking one of my breasts into his mouth.

Zephyr keeps running his hands down, gets to the hem of my pants and underwear, sliding them down, trailing his fingers down my legs. When he gets my pants and underwear to my ankle he lifts them gently pulling them all the way off. Lucas pulls himself off of my breast standing straight to look down in my eyes.

He grins, "You are delectable my dear. I think we need to cover you with our scent before we go into the lion's den. You know.... for protection," he says as he nips his mark on my neck, my arms dropping to his shoulders so I can put my fingers in his hair.

Zephyr bites my ass cheek, he glides his hands back up my body standing straight, "I think I told you to keep your hands up. You didn't listen," He smacks my ass hard, I bite my lip suppressing a moan.

Lucas bites his mark feeding on me, the moan I was trying to hide bursts out at the euphoric feeling. Zephyr licks his mark teasing it, sliding a hand between my leg playing with my clit. When Lucas has his fill he licks my neck sealing the bite, he kisses my neck gently pulling away from me. "Lay down Lilliana," he tells me as Zephyr pulls his fingers away.

Breathing heavy I lay into the center of the bed looking at both of the guys. Zephyr goes to the head of the bed grabbing one hand handcuffing it to the headboard above my head. Lucas does the same to the other one and grins looking down at me. "I think a couple orgasms will get you to behave. What do you think Z?"

"Sure, let's say...6 is the goal?" He looks to Lucas with a sly grin before looking back at me. "How about we play a game to make it more fun? I brought some toys from home to make things a little interesting. If you can guess who is doing things to you, then you can come. If not, we delay the pleasure trying again." He holds up a black mask that would cover my eyes completely.

"I think you are playing a losing game, I know you guys too well. But if you think you can trump me, by all means, I will accept the punishment." I say smiling biting my lip at the anticipation, my thighs pressing together.

They both laugh, "Sweetheart, we planned this well. The mask blocks your hearing too, when we tap your chin twice, that is when you make your guess." Lucas says pulling a duffle bag from under the bed.

I nod in agreement, Zephyr slips the mask over my eyes and ears, true to their word it blocks everything. I relax waiting.

I feel something tickling my stomach like a feather, I stifle a giggle squirming a little. A hand smacks my breast before using the feather-like object along my nipple making me squirm some more. 2 taps on my chin, I giggle squirming still, "Zephyr."

I get a kiss on my stomach trailing down to my pussy, *I must've gotten that right*. My legs are spread open as a mouth digs in, tongue sliding up and down from my clit to my core. I bite my lip arching my body, the tongue goes into my core as a finger swirls along my clit. A finger enters my pussy with the tongue pumping in and out.

Moaning I arch more, an orgasm gets close I can feel my body tremble. The touching disappears before I reach my peak and I groan at the loss of touch. "Damn it..." my body relaxes back against the mattress, I take a deep breath calming myself.

Something snaps on my stomach a little hard but not painful causing me to jolt biting my lip. It snaps again on my nipple sending a pleasurable shock to my core. I let out a heavy breath, it snaps the inside of my thigh making me moan out.

2 taps on my chin, "Shadow," I breath heavily. A kiss goes on my left mark, I moan in response. The mouth moves to my breasts biting, sucking on the nipples as a finger slips between my folds rubbing my clit. Biting my lip I arch towards the hand, the finger slips in pumping in and out, the thumb rubs my clit fast. Moaning I pull against the wrist restraints arching more, another finger slips in, pumping in and out faster, the mouth sucking on my nipple biting it occasionally.

My orgasm builds, my body trembling, but the hand and mouth doesn't stop. I come apart moaning loudly as I come all over the hand. I get another kiss on the left side of my neck breathing heavy as the fingers remove themselves from my core.

I take a couple deep breaths trying to slow my breathing, I feel a buzz on my nipple. Feels like silicone, *they are breaking out dildos...oh shit...* The dildo trails down my body slowly in the middle, rubs just outside my folds. I bite my lip tensing up, the dildo slips in rubbing against my clit, vibrating over it gently. 2 taps on my chin again, "Zephyr," I answer confidently. The dildo goes inside my core getting pulled in and out, a tongue flicks against my clit playing with it in circles.

It doesn't take long for another orgasm to build. I moan arching as it gets close, the dildo moves faster, the tongue swirling around my clit. I come moaning loud as my orgasm peaks, the dildo gets removed, and a kiss is placed on the right side of my neck.

I breathe heavily trembling, "I don't know if I can get to 6 guys, it's too much." I try to relax my breathing, a mouth meets mine kissing me deeply. I arch to it, my legs wrap around their waist, lining them up to my entrance. I can tell it is Zephyr by the size.

"Please Zephyr, please." I beg him, trying to pull him closer with my legs. He thrusts into me in one fluid movement, going back to kissing me deeply.

He thrusts in and out of me, hard but slow, I moan into his mouth tugging on the restraints. He moves to kissing my neck, his hand on my throat squeezing it thrusting a little faster. When I moan louder, he bites his mark thrusting harder and faster, it takes me over the edge, and I come undone. He thrusts into me hard coming inside me. He waits until I ride my orgasm out before pulling himself out, giving me a gentle kiss and gets off me so I can't feel him anymore.

My body gets flipped so my face is in the pillow, ass in the air. My body is propped so I am leaning my head against the headboard, my hands pressed against it. I get a hard smack to my ass making me jolt forward, I can feel when Lucas lines himself up, his hand taking a fist full of my hair pulling it back arching my body. "Shadow, please...take me."

I get a hard spank causing my body to arch again, my hair gets pulled a little before he slams into me hard. I moan out loudly, he lets go of my hair grabbing my neck pumping in and out hard and fast.

I scream out his name, moaning as he goes faster. He smacks my ass pounding me as fast as he can. He moves his hands to my breasts gripping them hard, using them to yank me backwards so he can thrust deeper. I moan loud breathing heavy, my orgasm gets close as my body trembles. He pinches my nipples hard twisting them still thrusting as fast as he can. I scream out, "Lucas!!" as I come all over his dick. He thrusts a couple more times before slamming all the way in coming inside me with a groan.

I slump against the headboard panting, he carefully pulls himself out and backs away. Without his support my body collapses. The mask gets removed and I cringe at the sudden light. Closing my eyes tight, I take slow breaths before slowly opening them blinking to get used to it.

Lucas releases my hands, helping me turn over so I can look at both of them. "How was that princess?" Zephyr asks, laying next to me.

"I am going to need a bath to relax my muscles before the ball." I stretch groaning. "It hurts so good though." I say with a smile looking to Lucas.

He gives me a huge grin, "Glad to hear sweetheart, think you can walk?"

I nod climbing out of bed stretching. I go into the bathroom, turn on the bath putting my hair in a bun to keep it dry. When the water fills to a level I'm happy with I climb in sitting down laying my head back. Zephyr takes a quick shower, followed by Lucas. I can hear them get dressed in the bedroom. I relax in the bath for a little bit before washing up. I get out of the bath, dry off wrapping the towel around my body. Pulling the bun loose off my head I fix my hair checking in the mirror. Satisfied I go back into the bedroom, the guys left and shut the door.

Good, they won't get a sneak peek this way. I slip the dress on, get the shoes strapped on, put on my jewelry and carry the mask in my hand. It's black with silver stars above the eyes. I put a fresh gloss on my lips and go to the mirror to see the finished look.
My heart stops, seeing the beautiful dress with the jewelry makes me smile. The dress is form fitting in the top, a slit down my right leg and flows behind me. The black has a slight shine to it causing the lace on top to stand out more.

You look amazing Lil, Arachne says proudly. Bellatrix adds in, *you look like a queen in her own right. Hold your head up high, OWN it.*

Thanks girls, I appreciate it, I reply back, taking a deep breath, I find Trix's daggers and slide them into the hidden sheaths along the slit of the dress strapping one to the thigh sheath she has. I know better than to be unprotected now.

Walking out of the room to find the guys, I see them standing by the door chatting. I walk to them slowly waiting for them to notice, it doesn't take long before Zephyr turns my way and taps Lucas's arm causing him to turn.

Chapter 20

Lilliana's POV

I hear their hearts hammer as I get closer, Zephyr is wearing a black tux with a blood red shirt and black tie. Lucas is wearing a silver tux with a black smokey design and a black shirt, his tie matching the tux with smoke.

They both bow when I reach them causing me to blush. "Don't do that," I say trying to pull them back up.

"Princess, I think I should start calling you Queen because you look like utter royalty tonight." Zephyr says taking my left hand kissing my rings.

My face heats more, "Sweetheart, you are divine." Lucas says kissing my rings as well. They both hold out an arm, I link my arms with them, and we leave the hotel room walking to the venue. I put my mask on tying it securely behind my head, the guys do the same. Zephyr's mask is blood red with black horns over his eyes, Lucas's is silver with black smoke around the eyes only.

We get to the front door, "Name?" the security guard asks roughly.

"Princess Lilliana Nightshade with my mates Lucas Bane and Zephyr Volos," I tell the guard causing him to fumble his clipboard.

He quickly bows opening the door for us, "Forgive me princess."

We step through, my grip tightening on the guy's arms. It's packed, people dancing, a band playing in the front, I see 3 thrones in the back of the room. As we walk in I feel eyes watching.

Breathe love, we are here with you, Lucas says through the bond.

I take a deep breath, we head towards the thrones. My parents are sitting on their thrones watching the dancer's enjoying themselves. The closer I get the more anxious I get.

The crowd parts letting us pass as people stare and whisper amongst themselves. We stand in front of the thrones. My parent's see us approach and my father stiffens in his seat, my mother's face darkens.

"Lilliana, is that you my dear?" My father asks as he stands giving me a fake smile.

I bow my head slightly but don't do more than that, "Yes father, I would never dare miss the family ball."

He moves towards us, "That makes me really pleased to hear." He notices Lucas and Zephyr, sees our arms linked together, a flicker of rage passes over his face. He gives another fake smile, "I see you brought Lucas, who is this other man you've brought?"

"Zephyr Volos," I say smiling despite the fear I feel inside.

"Why did you bring them? Surely one man is enough." He says with a slight sneer and judgmental tone.

Bellatrix starts to get angry, I take a deep breath trying to keep myself calm. *Trix, I've got this, please don't interfere,* I tell her smiling at our father. "These are my mates, and my fiancés. They came to support me and introduce themselves."

My mother finally walks up, "That's a bold face lie Lilliana. You're being shameful. There is no such thing as multiple mates."

Zephyr puts his hand on top of mine resting on his arm, "Actually Mrs. Nightshade, there is. It's rare but it does happen. We are her mates, she bares both of our marks, and we bare hers."

My mother steps closer to look at my neck seeing both marks, as well as the hickeys the guys left before we got to the ball. She stumbles backward falling into my father's arms. "If you will excuse us, we are going to find a table. We are getting a little hungry," Lucas says leading us away from my parents.

We find an empty table, I sit down, my body trembles slightly as I breathe, slowly trying to rid the anxiety building inside. Lucas sits on my left, Zephyr kisses the top of my head and leans down to my ear so I can hear him through the music and crowd, "I'll go get some food, don't leave Lucas' side."

I give him a nod, Lucas puts an arm on the back of my chair rubbing my back softly with his finger. I smile at him, "Well that could've gone worse," I say leaning towards him.

"True, maybe we can have a pleasant time," he says leaning closer to me. "You have a lot of admirers it looks like," he nudges his head to the crowd of people in front of us, they keep looking at us occasionally whispering.

Lisa comes up to the table smiling brightly when she sees us. "Princess Lilli, you look amazing!" She gets closer to me, I stand giving her a hug. She rubs my back before whispering into my ear, "Don't take your parent's words to heart. They are wrong. You are not shameful, wear your mate's mark with pride my dear."

Sniffling I hug her close, "Thank you Lisa, I appreciate it."

Lucas stands holding a hand out to Lisa, she takes it, but he just flips it over and bows, kissing her hand. "You did a magnificent job turning this princess into a queen. I am forever in your debt."

She blushes but her smile doesn't fade. "I would do anything for this girl. I made her outfits for every occasion for many years, I hated how her parents and Alpha Lennix treated her. Thank you for making her happy."

"She made us happy first, especially when she agreed to marry us." Lucas tells her, standing up straight and wrapping his arm around my shoulder.

Zephyr comes up with food, setting it down when he sees Lisa. "Ms. Lisa, glad to see you." He gives her a curt bow before giving her a hug. "Your handiwork is unparalleled. I almost had a heart attack when I first saw her."

"Well, you two clean up just as nice as she does. Women just have more charm," she says winking at me. "I won't keep you, I wanted to see my handiwork and make sure you kids liked it. Lilli my dear, don't be a stranger." She kisses my cheek giving the guys a hug before walking away from the table.

Sitting back down I eat quietly, the guys eat slower and looking around occasionally. When we finish our food Lucas gets up to put the plates in the bin, *Babe I need to wash my hands, some stuff spilled out I will be back shortly*, Lucas tells me through the bond. I pass the message to Zephyr looking at him with a smile.

He leans towards me and gives me a soft kiss stroking my knee. "I wish I could rip this dress off you so bad right now," he whispers into my ear.

I stifle a giggle, we get interrupted by Lennix pushing Zephyr out of his chair. "Don't kiss my fiancé dickhead," he yells out.

I stand quickly trying to shove Lennix out of the way so I can help Zephyr, "I'm not your fiancé anymore Len!"

Lennix pushes me backwards causing me to stumble, a guard grabs my arms pinning them to the side. Zephyr stands up quickly, he punches Lennix square in the jaw causing him to falter. Zephyr sees the guard holding me and makes his way to us.

The guard backs up pulling me with him, "Let me go!" I yell out loudly. He puts his hand over my mouth to keep me from talking.

BELLATRIX! I scream into my head urging her to take over.

Bellatrix's POV

I jump through the door pulling Lilli back, I bite the guard's hand hard hearing the bone crack. The guard screams out shoving me forward into Zephyr's chest.

Lennix comes up behind Zephyr stabbing a fork into his shoulder. Zephyr yells out in pain, turning to face Lennix keeping me behind him. *Lucas! We need you!!! Where are you?!* I scream down the bond.

Lennix kicks Zephyr hard in the stomach, swings his fist towards his face. Zephyr blocks the punch and delivers his own, landing in Lennix's stomach.

I feel something off, so I look around, I see a figure in the rafters loading a crossbow. They fire the bolt towards me, I dodge it easily. My parent's come up behind me, my father wraps his arms around me roughly. I slam my head back into his face, but his hold gets tighter.

I growl when I see Lennix pull out a knife from his pocket. He slices at Zephyr, but he manages to dodge it. My father whispers into my ear, "Watch your mate die you whore."

I yell as loud as I could, my arms lighting on fire burning my father. He quickly lets go scrambling backwards. I jump towards Lennix and Zephyr, kicking the knife Lennix held out of his hand. He growls at me, I pull a dagger from the dress throwing it at him and nicking his shoulder.

He stumbles back holding his arm. I look to the figure in the rafters, they are loading another bolt. I fling another dagger in their direction hitting them in the thigh causing them to fall. They disappear into a cloud of purple smoke.

I grab Zephyr's hand, pulling him behind me my arms still on fire. I make sure the flames don't burn him, he rips the fork from his shoulder tossing it onto the floor, "We need to get out of here. There are too many innocents that can get hurt, where's Lucas?" he asks backing up pulling me with him.

"I don't know, I called for him, but I didn't get anything back." We slowly back out of the building, we run to the car getting in quickly and he speeds off.

"Maybe he got ambushed as well, went home waiting for us," he suggest driving as fast as possible.

I hear my phone go off, I open it and see Sedrick messaged me. A photo of Lucas is seen, he seems knocked out, tied up, and covered in blood.

"NO!!" I yell out, Zephyr looks at my phone, and his hand tightens on the shifter and steering wheel. We pull into the house skidding to a stop.

I read the message under the photo, "If you want your mate back alive, you will stop fighting. You have to choose which mate you can live without. Kill Volos or we kill your precious shadow. I'll give you one week. King Julian Nightshade." Lilli screams in our head making it feel like it's going to explode, she falls into sobs as she goes into her room sealing herself off.

I rush out of the car screaming loudly. The trees near us go up in flames. Zephyr comes up behind me wrapping his arms around me. I fall to my knees, putting the fire out. "I'm going to get him back..." I say looking at the gravel in front of me, "I'm going to kill them all."

Zephyr holds me tight, "I'll help. We will get him back, I swear." I look up at the full moon shining brightly above us.

Epilogue
Lucas's POV

Why am I so cold, why is it so dark, where am I? I ask myself feeling my eyes open, it's pitch black. What happened?

I try to touch my head but can feel chains restricting my movement. Am I chained up like an animal? I kick my legs, but they don't budge shackled to the surface I'm on.

I scream out but it just echoes right back. I close my eyes trying to remember what happened.

I cleaned the table of the plates, went to the bathroom. Sedrick came up behind me a glazed-over look in his eyes, 4 guards came in with him. The guards tackle me into the floor kicking and punching me every chance they could get.
I lay there bleeding, coughing up blood and look up to Sedrick who hasn't moved yet. He comes to me and sticks a needle into the side of my neck. Everything slowly fades to black as I black out.
Lilliana…Zephyr, keeping my eyes closed I reach through the mate bond trying to find Lilli. I can't feel anything, it's like I'm being blocked. I scream in frustration and pull against the chains.

I'll get out of here Lilli, I'll be back soon, I promise my love.

Bonus Scene

Julian Nightshade's POV (After Lucas' departure)

I look at Chelsea considering her words previously, *it makes sense, but there is risk involved when trying to depend on Lennix.* Nodding I speak up, "Do what you can to get close to her. Try to fix the curse before she gets marked. I highly doubt it is the abomination, so target the other one."

Lennix looks to me with a grin, "She will lose her mind if we go after the hybrid. She talked about him all the time."

"We can plan something for her birthday, like I said, he can't be her mate. When he transitioned he was a friend, nothing more. I say kill the other one, take Lucas, and force her submission." I address the group, sitting back into my chair. Chelsea stands from her chair, the man at her feet jumps up standing next to her. "I will get something scheduled with her soon, and report back quickly." They leave, Lennix sits back in his chair watching me and my mate.

"Now that the extra ears are gone, what are we going to do about my cousin?" Lennix speaks quickly, his nerves showing clearly.

I raise my eyebrow at him, "No one can guarantee death from a forced transition. When I murdered his parents I tried to find him. We forced a transition because assassination works better when there is a story behind it. I took him in to keep him close by, it was wrong of me to assume he lost his wolf. It was an oversight I don't plan to make again." I tap my desk a couple times thinking, "Don't worry Lennix, he does not know his lineage, therefore your father still thinks he is dead. If we lock him away, hidden with no escape...you will still become King when your father steps down. It may be Lucas Bane's birthright, however his parents became my enemy so I chose you instead. Do...Not...Fail...Me." I say with as much venom and intimidation as possible. Lennix pales, nodding quickly.

Author Note

Thank you for reading this story. Stay tuned for more, I am really excited to continue this journey. This story could not have been possible without support from those closest to me, my fiancé Josh, and my best friends Phillip and Sharon. I really appreciate all the help you guys have given to make this suit my writing style and give it more life.

Being an indie writer is a journey I have always wanted to take. Don't miss out on the next book, it is already in the works!!